IN THE END

ELISABETH MCSPARREN

MILTON & HUGO L.L.C.
4407 Park Ave., Suite 5
Union City, NJ 07087, USA

Website: *www.miltonandhugo.com*
Hotline: *1- 888-778-0033*
Email: *info@miltonandhugo.com*

Ordering Information:
Quantity sales. Special discounts are granted to corporations, associations, and other organizations. For more information on these discounts, please reach out to the publisher using the contact information provided above.

Library of Congress Control Number: 2024919526
ISBN-13:   979-8-89285-278-4   [Paperback Edition]
                  979-8-89285-277-7   [Digital Edition]

Rev. date: 07/29/2024

CONTENTS

INTRODUCTION

Stark:

"Saylor!" I yelled, watching her and two bodyguards take her onto a private airplane.

She looked back at me with a smile and then howled.

"I'm gonna miss her," Carly, her best friend, who looked more like her twin, whispered.

"We all are," Rachel, the leader of the group, put her arms around us.

"She was the scariest one out of all of us…" Lola, the youngest of us all, started to cry. I didn't think it would get worse from there, but it did.

"Stark! It's time to go home and pack up. We're moving!" I heard my mom from behind us.

"We'll keep in touch?" I asked the girls, they were the only thing left that I had of Saylor. Them and my sister who adored Saylor, of course it wasn't always the best idea to look up to her though.

"Of course. We got in touch with her brother, she's staying with him." Rachel nodded in confirmation.

"Thank you, take care girls." I gave a small smile, turned and walked away towards my mom in the car.

"You better hide those tears before we get home and your dad sees." My mom warned.

"Yeah, yeah, I know." I rolled my hazelnut eyes at her.

"Don't give me that. We both know that your dad doesn't like you crying," She glared at me.

In response, I just sighed and looked out the window, thinking about how much I love her and would end up missing her.

— Half A Year Later —

"Why did we have to move here again?" I asked my mom as she drove up to my new school.

"Because this is where your father's new mission is," my mom explained.

"And you're still with him because...?" I wondered.

"Not now Stark, get to class. I'll see you later, I love you." My mom sighed, my dad was a rough conversation for her, he was a man I never wanted to be.

"Fine," I sighed back, grabbing my bag and getting out of the car. "I love you too mom." I closed the door and then walked up to the school, realizing I didn't know where I was going.

"Excuse me, you need help?" A quiet girl's voice came up from behind me.

"Yeah, I think so," I gave a small chuckle and turned around. "Damn..."

"Huh?" She looked at me surprised, half smiling.

"Sorry," I gulped. I couldn't hide the fact that she looked like my Saylor, but I was probably seeing things because of how much I missed her.

"It's fine," she smiled. "What can I help you with?"

"Finding the office possibly?" I asked.

"Yeah, come this way," she waved her hand to follow. I followed her to the office and it already seemed that the office knew her quite well.

"Bella, what do you need?" The office attendant asked.

"Do you already want to go home?" Another office member asked.

"No, not yet. I'm just bringing a new student here." She gave a small laugh with an eye roll from her vibrant orange eyes.

"Well, that's good to hear," the office member smiled and then went back to work.

"Miss Sasha is in her office?" She wondered to the office attendant.

"Yes," the office attendant nodded, then glanced at me. "What's your name?"

"Stark Hunt." I proudly said.

"I'll be right back, I trust Ms. Backabee to get you everything you need." Bella, the beautiful girl turned to me.

"Okay," I shrugged.

"Alright here is your schedule. I'm sure Bella will help you with whatever you need," Ms. Backabee smiled. "Take good care of her, and try to keep her out of the office.

"Ok?" I answered hesitantly, luckily for me Bella came back and was able to look at my schedule.

"How lucky we are, we have some classes together," she looked up and smiled.

"Cool, do you think you can show me where homeroom is?" I wondered.

"Yes, of course. Mrs. Evergreen is our math teacher, we have her at the end of the day, but you have her for homeroom." Bella explained.

"Wow, Miss Bella, this is the most I've seen you socialize with someone besides us," a different office lady came over to us.

"Haha, Miss Sasha," Bella rolled her eyes.

"You better get going before you both are late," Miss Sasha suggested.

"Planned on, see you guys later!" She waved and we started to walk out of the building.

"Hopefully not," we heard from both Ms. Backabee and Miss Sasha.

"Hey, so I've got two questions for you," I told her, walking up next to her.

"Yeah?" She looked over at me, "what are they?"

"Do you happen to be related to Saylor Martez?" I asked.

"Sorry, I don't recognize that name, so I don't think so," her energy level changed from a high to a low quickly. "What's the next question?"

"Oh, um, Ms. Backabee told me to try to keep you out of the office?"

"Don't worry about it," Bella automatically shut that down, she was acting a little strange or different from before. "Well, this is your homeroom, I'll see you around."

"Wait, what about my other classes?" I grabbed her arm before she walked away. "Sorry," I mumbled and let go.

"You're fine," she gave a small smile and gave me directions to the rest of my classes before she left.

"Thanks," I sighed before heading into my classroom. When I arrived, I talked to my teacher, Mrs. Evergreen, who explained a few things and then gave me a desk to sit at. Soon after, a kid came in howling and sat next to me. Of course this day couldn't get any worse,

I already have Bella making me think of Saylor, and now this kid is howling.

"Landon, we discussed this, come in quietly next time," Mrs. Evergreen looked at the kid next to me long and hard.

"Alright, alright," he waved her off then turned towards me. "Yo man! You must be the new kid, I'm Landon."

"Yeah, I'm Stark, nice to meet you," I smiled.

The rest of the day went by fast, I didn't see Bella until math. However, I learned that Landon and I had every class together, which was nice to know that I had at least one friend at the school. When it came to math, Bella came in late and I didn't get the chance to talk to her. Every so often, I'd look over at her; one of the times, Landon caught me and shook his head.

"She's weird and really different," he whispered.

"I don't think she's weird, she was nice to me earlier," I whispered back.

"Dude! She has orange eyes!" He exclaimed quietly.

"So? My last girlfriend had orange eyes; then again, she was very unique." I told him.

"Huh, I've never seen anyone with orange eyes before. But was she hot?" Landon asked.

"She was much more than hot, she was gorgeous. She intimidated everyone at our school," I gave a small laugh, soon holding back tears that I couldn't bear to shed.

"I'm sorry man, you must miss her," he frowned.

"I do. I miss her so damn much, she was my life," I nodded. I soon noticed Bella was looking over at me with a slight smile. As soon as I looked over at her, she looked away.

When school was out, I ran over to Bella and asked for her number. Surprisingly she said yes and gave it to me, then said goodbye. Once I found where my mom was parked, I got in the car and mentioned that I was going to marry Bella.

"But what about Saylor?" My younger sister Mia asked.

"Yeah, I know. But, there's something about Bella that's different. Plus, I've gotta move on one way or another." I explained with a sigh.

"I'm sorry, brother." Mia gave me a hug from the back seat of the car.

"It's okay Mia, can't do anything about it,"

Two months passed, and I hadn't seen Bella since the first day I started school. We texted, but I hadn't seen her since. It wasn't until I got into a fight and won with a bloody nose during lunch that she kept her time in the office.

"Bella?!" I exclaimed in shock, even though I shouldn't have because the office ladies tried to get me to keep her out of the office.

"Oh my gosh! Stark! What did you do?!" She turned and gasped.

"Might've gotten into a fight, but hey, I won," I shrugged.

"Stark!" She grumbled in frustration. It was strange, I didn't know why she was acting like this. The last time I saw a girl like this it was Saylor, and that was because I got into a fist fight with my dad and nearly broke my hand.

"Bella?" I questioned, looking closer at her.

"Sorry," she gave a slight laugh, it was like a switch turned off or something. "Let's get your nose taken care of."

"Okay," I was still confused but followed her into the nurses office. "Is this where you go?"

She smiled and answered, "yeah. Miss Sasha is basically my best friend."

"What about me?!" I teased, feeling offended.

"You hang out with Landon and his little group. They think I'm weird and I don't think they like me." She explained.

I took a deep breath and watched her as she attended to my nose. She seemed patient and very much so calm, plus pretty as well.

"Will you go out with me?" It might have not been the right time, but the words just slipped out.

She cleared her throat before asking, "why?"

"Because, you remind me of someone," I told her.

"If I remind you of someone; then I don't think I should say yes," she threw the gauze into the trash and crossed her arms. She was still a few inches away from me, close enough that it was hard not to have the impulse control to reach out and kiss her.

"Please Bella, please?" I started to beg, holding every inch of myself from grabbing her and pulling her in.

◆————————◆————————◆

"Bella, mind answering the question?" Mrs. Evergreen asked. I watched as the quiet girl, Bella, took a deep breath in then out.

"No, but may I see the nurse? I'm not doing so well," she wondered.

"I suppose," Mrs. Evergreen sighed and let Bella leave the classroom.

"How does she get away with that?" My man, Landon, whispered to me.

"I don't know man, maybe you should try it?" I suggested, shaking my head, worrying a little bit about Bella.

"Will do," he nodded and raised his hand in the air.

"Mr. Landon? You want to try answering the question?" Mrs. Evergreen looked surprised, and hell, I didn't blame her. Landon was a kid who fit the "cool kid" stereotype.

"No ma'am, but I was wondering if I could use the restroom?" He glanced at me, a smile on his face.

"After we solve this problem," Mrs. Evergreen shook her head and began helping Landon with the math problem.

"Backfire," he mouthed at me.

"Sorry man," I frowned, not realizing I got caught.

"Stark, why don't you join us too," Mrs. Evergreen smiled.

"Um, I think I'm good, thank you," I politely declined.

"Why don't you join us anyways," Mrs. Evergreen insisted.

"Okay," I sighed, this was not my plan.

Soon after Bella came back in and looked straight at me. I wished I could go up and give her a hug and see how she was. But I couldn't because she wanted to keep us a little secret because of rumors, but I also think she was scared as well…

Bella/Saylor:

I was upstairs in my room on a FaceTime call with my best friends Carly, Rachel, and Lola when everything changed.

"You're serious right?!" Lola cried out.

"Yes," I laughed.

"It can't be that bad right? You guys hang out all the time," Carly added.

"I can see it," Rachel mumbled.

"Oooo, Rachel and Lola..." I started.

"Heyyy," Lola laughed, looking a little embarrassed.

"Wait, what was that noise?" I asked, looking out my doorway, hearing someone break down the door. Then I heard soft foot prints cross my room.

"What noise?" Rachel wondered.

"Hang on, be quiet. I wanna know what's happening." I whispered, they nodded in response.

I took my phone and tip-toed to my doorway. I went to an army crawl position and started to crawl my way to the edge of the wall, seeing my two little sisters by the top of the staircase.

"What are you girls doing?!" I whispered.

"We heard the door get broken down," Alexis whispered, holding on to Ella. It was easy to tell that they were scared, after all they were seven, but even I was scared as well.

"Okay, I'll handle this," I gave a comforting smile and took a closer look. I looked out the front door and noticed a police car. *What's going on?* I thought.

I then turned on my excellent hearing, a power I gained at thirteen and took a closer look at what was going on.

"I don't know what you're talking about," my father mumbled.

"We know who you are. We'd like to see your girls," one of the strangers said, in a stern way.

"No." My mom said sternly and very protectively.

"If you don't let us see them, we'll have to murder you both and find your little girls." Another guy threatened.

I looked down at my phone, seeing my friend's faces in shock. Lola and I were both on the rim of tears while Rachel and Carly were angry. I looked over at my twin sisters who also looked terrified. I didn't blame them at all. I didn't even have to turn on my excellent hearing to hear the conversation, they were loud enough already.

I looked back at my phone and told them, "I love you girls. Tell Stark I love him too," I mouthed and hung up.

I looked over at Alexis and Ella and gave them my phone. I told them to call the agency while I distracted the strangers. They nodded as they took my phone and ran to the otherside of the hallway. I nodded and sighed. It might be the last time I see those two. Once I heard my mom cry out I quickly and quietly walked down the stairs and turned to the left where three strangers stood. Their backs were towards me and my parents were backed up against the wall facing me. My parents were terrified, even if it looked like my dad was putting on a brave face.

"I'm right here." I cleared my throat, trying to get myself as strong and ready as possible, even if my voice was a little shaky.

The men turned around to face me, creepy smiles appearing on their faces, "well hello Saylor. Where are the twins?"

"How-how do you know my name?" I gulped soon adding, "they're normal, nothing like us."

Everything happened so fast. One of the guys grabbed my arm and my parents used their power to fight back. Like Superman, my family has their kryptonite, geneolise. It was an antidote that made it so we couldn't use our powers. It made us very weak, and could sometimes make us pass out. Even though my parents were running all over the place trying to attack the guys, the guys were able to catch them both and input the geneolise. Since my parents no longer had the advantage to use their powers, the men had the advantage to shoot them both.

"No!" I screamed, tears running down my face.

— Half A Year Later —

"Ella and Alexis miss us," my older brother Andrew told me as he drove up to the new school I went to.

"You're lucky you get to hear from them," I rolled my eyes.

"Hey, do you have a new student coming today?" Andrew asked. I thought he was trying to change the subject until I saw who he was pointing to.

"Is that...?" My voice trailed off, unable to compute what was going on. "It can't be..."

"Only one way to find out, Sis," Andrew looked over at me. "What are you going to do if it is him?"

"Keep my cover. I have no choice." I answered, even though I didn't like the fact that I had to hide my identity from my best friend.

"You gonna be ok?" He asked.

"I hope so, we'll see if anything's changed." I gave a small smile.

"Call me if you need anything, I love you." Andrew rubbed my shoulder.

"Thanks, love you too." I sighed getting out of the car.

Stark being Stark seemed lost, I was lucky that nobody was around so I wasn't afraid to approach him.

"Excuse me, do you need help?" I asked, being forced to keep my cover.

"Yeah, I think so." he gave a small chuckle and turned towards me. "Damn."

"Huh?" I half smiled, being surprised that he thought I was attractive. My appearance from the last time he saw me changed a great deal that it was hard to even recognize my old self.

"Sorry," I heard him gulp, looking a little sad.

"It's fine," I smiled then got to the point. "What can I help you with?"

"Finding the office possibly?" He wondered.

"Yeah, come this way," I waved for him to follow. Once I got into the office I was waiting for the expected comments or questions.

"Bella, what do you need?" Ms. Backabee asked.

"Do you already want to go home?" Miss Perky wondered.

I laughed and rolled my eyes, answering, "No, not yet. I'm just bringing a new student here."

"Well, that's good to hear," Miss Perky smiled, going back to work.

"Miss Sasha is in her office?" I guessed looking over at Ms. Backabee.

"Yes," she nodded, then glanced at Stark. "What's your name?"

"Stark Hunt." He proudly said.

"I'll be right back, I trust Ms. Backabee to get you everything you need." I turned towards Stark and made sure I got the okay before I left. I then walked off to see Miss Sasha, my best friend and cousin.

"Bella, school just started, do you want to go home already?" Miss. Sasha frowned.

"No," I sighed, sitting on the little bed. "It's something else."

"Oh? What is it?" She wondered, a little concern in her voice.

"Remember Stark?"

"Your old boyfriend?"

"Yeah, well, he's going to this school now. And I have no idea on what to do." I explained, feeling a little helpless. The old me would have never felt this way before.

"You need to keep your cover Bella. I betcha you want to tell him," she told me.

"I do, and I know. It's just hard," I sighed.

"I know, I'm sorry. But you should probably go see him now," Miss. Sasha gave a slight smile.

"Yeah, I should." I nodded and headed back to Stark. Once I was there I noticed that we had a few of the same classes. "How lucky we are, we have some classes together," I smiled.

"Cool, do you think you can show me where homeroom is?" He asked.

"Yes, of course. Mrs. Evergreen is our math teacher, we have her at the end of the day but you have her for homeroom," I explained.

"Wow, Miss. Bella, this is the most I've seen you socialize with someone besides us," Miss. Sasha teased, coming over to us.

"Haha, Miss. Sasha," I rolled my eyes.

"You better get going before you both are late," she suggested.

"Planned on, see you guys later!" I waved, heading out of the office, hoping that Stark would follow.

"Hopefully not," we heard from both Ms. Backabee and Miss Sasha. Yeah, right, I gave a small laugh thinking to myself that the office ladies and I knew that I was going to see them later.

"Hey, so I've got two questions for you," Stark ran up to catch me.

"Yeah?" I looked over at him, "what are they?"

"Do you happen to be related to Saylor Martez?" He asked. The question shouldn't have caught me off guard, Saylor and Bella both have the same but different attributes to each other. Unfortunately, I couldn't stay in my own head so I had to answer.

"Sorry, I don't recognize that name, so I don't think so," I lied, being on the brim of tears. Then I remembered that he had another question, "what's the next question?"

"Oh, um, Ms. Backabee told me to try to keep you out of the office?"

"Of course she did," I muttered to myself.

"Don't worry about it." I stated, no longer wanting to talk anymore. "Well, this is your homeroom and math class. I'll see you later"

"Wait, what about my other classes?" I felt him grab my arm as I was starting to walk away. "Sorry," he let go of my arm as I looked back.

"You're fine," I gave a small smile and then told him directions to his other classes.

Two months passed and I avoided Stark at all cost, except when it came down to texting. It was easier texting him than being seen in public with him, he already got teased by Landon about me, especially on his first day. I missed my old school when I didn't care much about that stuff, hell, nobody was talking like that, course, I ran the school. But, it wasn't until I was eating lunch in Miss Sasha's office telling her about how Stark and I are doing that I saw Stark from the window and ran over.

"Bella?!" He exclaimed as he saw me.

"Oh my gosh! Stark! What did you do?!" I gasped.

"Might've gotten into a fight. But, hey, I won," he shrugged.

"Stark!" I shook my head at him, disappointed.

"Bella?" He questioned, snapping me out of my Saylor side that I've hid so well from him.

"Sorry," I gave a small laugh. "Let's get your nose taken care of."

"Okay," he mumbled. "Is this where you go?"

I smiled and answered, "yea. Miss. Sasha is basically my best friend."

"What about me?!" He teased, acting all offended.

"You hang out with Landon and his little group. They think I'm weird and I don't think they like me." I explained, in fact I know that they don't like me and that they think I'm weird.

What Stark said next surprised me, but at the same time didn't either. "Will you go out with me?"

I cleared my throat and kept my eyes on the bloody nose, "why?"

"Because, you remind me of someone," He told me.

"If I remind you of someone; then I don't think I should say yes," I finished up and stood in the same place as when I was attending to his nose, just standing up straight.

"Please Bella, please?" He begged, playing with all my heart strings.

I had to get out of that classroom. I had to get away from the stares and the little mutters that would follow after I answered the question correctly. I went to the nurses office and when I got there, Miss Sasha gave me a disappointing look. Everyone at the school knew her by her first name, she loved being called by her first name.

"Bella, this is the eighth time you're coming here this week. What's wrong this time?" Miss Sasha wondered.

"It's the stares and mutters. And it feels so closed in and I can't get air," I complained, " well, I can, but it's not fresh."

"Either call your brother or go back to class," she sighed.

"I can't stay here with you?"

"Bella, we may be cousins, but I have a job to do and you should be in class if you aren't actually not feeling well."

"But I'm not feeling well. I'm now getting bullied to the point where I want to fight people again Sasha,"

"Bella.." She started until she looked at my puppy eyes. "Call your brother, that's the least I can do."

"Yes ma'am." I nodded, pulling out my phone to call my brother.

As I pulled out my phone, I noticed I got a few messages from Stark.

> Stark: *How did you get out of answering the question? And are you okay?*
> Stark: *Dang it! Teach' caught me texting. Text me back when schools out kay?*

I shook my head with a sigh and went to call Andrew.
"Hello?" He answered.

"Hey, I'm not doing so well. Could you come and pick me up? Please," I asked.

I heard a sigh coming from the other side of the phone. "Fine, I'll be there in ten."

"Thank you."

"You're welcome, bye." With that he hung up and I looked up at Miss Sasha

"Andrew will be here in ten."

"Go ahead and go back to class to grab your stuff. Andrew should be here by the time you get back,"

"Okay," I nodded making my way out.

Once I got outside I took a big deep breath into the fresh spring air. When I made my way back to class I looked all the way back to where Stark sat. Stark looked miserable until our eyes met and a hopeful smile came across his face with hazelnut eyes lightning up. I gave a small smile with blush filling my cheeks.

We're dating, but we haven't put a label on it. I don't want to go public to the school because there would still be more rumors than there already are between the two of us. I only say that because Landon and his group of friends make fun of me and Stark always defends me and then he gets teased about it. It makes me feel bad about that, and makes me want to show my true self more, but I can't because I need to protect myself and my sisters.

"Bella?" I heard Mrs. Evergreen say, I blinked a couple of times then I looked over at her. I heard a few kids giggle and snicker, making my Bella side embarrassed, but also enraged from Saylor.

"Um, I'm going home," Bella's side mumbled, rushing to my desk and grabbing my stuff. I was about to leave and then Mrs. Evergreen called my name.

"Bella,"

"Yeah?" I turned towards her.

"Miss Sasha told me to suggest that you should stay home tomorrow? With the amount of times you've been going in there?" She suggested on behalf of Sasha.

"Of course," I muttered to myself. Then aloud, "hopefully, if my family lets me."

"I'm coming over," I heard from Stark, who whispered. I looked back at him trying to give a reassuring smile, although I nearly ended up crying.

Once I left the classroom I walked towards the office to where Andrew was walking towards me.

"Sasha said we didn't have to go in, are you ready?" He asked once I got up to him.

"Yeah," I answered.

"Well then, let's go," he sighed.

"Andrew?" I looked up at him as we walked to the car.

"What?" He huffed.

"I'm sorry," I mumbled knowing he could hear me.

"Sis, why do you tell me that you want to go to school, but once you get there, you want to leave?" He asked, a little worried.

I sighed and shifted my eyes back to the ground. "So I can see Stark and he knows I'm okay."

"What's the harm in telling him you're not okay? It wasn't always like this," he questioned, unlocking the car and getting in.

"I'm different now Andrew. Being Bella for a while now isn't the same as acting like her. I'm permanently Bella now and it fucking sucks. I'm barely the other girl I used to be and it's not like I can tell anybody about it. I have a cover to keep, that doesn't just affect me, but also the twins." I explained, "Stark will end up worrying and I don't need that. Especially since he'll want to be around me the whole time, most importantly at school, and that's not needed."

"Saylor...." He started. There was no need to apologize, we both knew how hard this was on me. So instead of talking about half of it he said, "Nobody likes rumors. I know we both dealt with that. But, he probably will want to be around you because he cares about you."

I looked out the car window, tears almost forming, "I'll tell him when he comes over."

"Sasha told me you should stay home tomorrow," Andrew glanced over at me.

My mood snapped fast, "No. I'm fine."

"Woah, chill," Andrew gasped. Soon adding, "And clearly you're not."

"Sorry, everyone has been telling me that. And I don't need to stay home," I concluded not wanting to cry at all.

"Saylor…" He repeated, even more empathetic. There was no point in hiding them now.

"I just wish…" I sniffled, "that I could have protected them."

"You protected Alexis and Ella," Andrew reminded me.

"That's not enough! We don't even get to see them!" I cried out.

"I know," he sighed. "Is there anything the teachers or I can do?"

"Let Stark and I sit next to each other? It's the only normality I have, and it has to be discrete and not like we asked to sit next to each other." I answered.

"I'll see what I can do," he gave a small smile.

"Thanks," I gave one back.

"Taylor missed you this morning. She was upset when Sabrina had to wake her up."

"Oh? I guess I'll have to make it up to her then."

Andrew and I were six years apart. He got married to Sabrina, his high school sweetheart soon after graduation. They soon had a daughter, Taylor who is now four, my niece.

Sabrina works at Starbucks and goes to college in the evenings, she is working on getting her degree in nursing. Andrew is a stay at home dad while he tries to get a degree in criminal justice online.

Sabrina's dad, Mr. Leon helped buy them a nice two story house, it almost looks like a mansion. Especially with how many rooms there were.

"Sis, we're home," Andrew's voice startled me to where I jumped, making him laugh.

"Not funny," I grumbled unbuckling. I walked to the door then stopped.

"What?" Andrew asked, looking over at me.

"Is Sabrina home or did you leave your four year old daughter, who you watch over like a hawk, home by herself?" I wondered.

"Yeah, I left her home alone, but she was out like a light, and I couldn't wake her up." He sighed, I could tell he felt like he didn't like the choice he made.

"Hey, I can hear her breathing. Still sounds like she's sleeping, I know you can hear her too." I soothed with a comforting smile.

"Thanks, now let's get inside," he smiled back.

We walked up to the door, and once Andrew unlocked and opened the door; I saw a sleeping Taylor curled up on the living room couch. Putting my stuff down I smiled and walked over to her placing my warm lips against her cold forehead, making her wake up.

"Auntie Bella!" She cheered diving on me, making us crash to the floor.

"Ahh," I laughed rolling her to her back and harassing her with kisses while she giggled.

"You owe me," she sat up and crossed her arms along with pouting as well.

"What do I owe you?" I wondered.

"I get to sleep with you!" She announced.

"Oh, pumpkin, I don't think that's gonna happen. I'm sorry," my face fell apologizing.

"Why not?" She whined.

"Taylor, no whining," Andrew told her sternly, in response she nodded.

"Your daddy is making me do something huge and knowing him, I don't know what he would do.." I explained giving a slight frown.

"Hey, it's for the better." Andrew then looked at me sternly.

"Yeah, and hopefully it doesn't kill me again," I rolled my eyes, Saylor coming out.

"Starky's coming over," her deep sky blue eyes brightened up as happiness and blush crossed her face.

"I can't believe you have a crush on my boyfriend," my own eyes went big as soon as I realized what I said, shit. As Bella, I'd never say those words but as Saylor, it didn't matter what I said, there was nothing surprising about it.

"You and Starky are together!!" Taylor lit up with excitement as she stood on the couch and danced around.

"Wow, never thought I'd hear those words," Andrew sounded surprised by Bella's choice of not thinking. I looked up at him where he was standing behind the couch a few feet away against the doorway of the kitchen.

"Pumpkin," I started but got interrupted by the doorbell.

"Come on Sweetpea, help me clean up the kitchen," Andrew went over to Taylor who was still dancing around. He grabbed her by the waist and pulled her into his arms as he walked off with a giggling, happy girl.

I sighed as the doorbell rang once more followed by, "come on babe, open up."

"Coming!" I yelled getting off the floor and walking over to the door. When I opened the door he came in and closed the door and then grabbed me for a hug, squeezing me tightly.

"Are you okay? What's going on? There's got to be something." He muttered into my shoulder. His warm breath sent shock waves all through my body. I smiled and hugged him tightly back.

"I'm fine, I do have to talk to you though," I pulled away and gave a slight reassuring smile. I wasn't too surprised to see worry and concern all over his face though.

I took his hand and went up the stairs that were right across the door. Once we were all the way up the stairs we walked past Taylor's two rooms, her bed room and then her playroom, along with her bathroom right across. After her two rooms there was my room, like Taylor's bathroom; my bathroom was across from my room.

"Sorry for the mess," I mumbled embarrassed about how messy my room was. Clothes, mostly jeans, were on my floor. Balled up paper on my floor, my bed wasn't made, blankets, pillows, and my important stuffed animals all over my room. To top off how messy my room was, my drawers from both my desk and dresser were open along with my closet door being open and my many pairs of shoes were a mess on the floor.

"I never knew Bella would have such a messy room, she always seemed so organized," Stark teased. I snorted and gave a small eye roll. I finished picking up some of my stuff to make it more 'clean'. I closed my mirror and stood in front of it.

I looked at myself remembering who I once looked like. Trying to get rid of the insecurities Bella had, not that my Saylor side had any.

The one thing that didn't change about what we loved so much were the curves, height, and not much acne. They both didn't like the phoenix tattoo that had to be hidden, even during the summer time. Bikinis were always a no, even at my own house. The orange eyes always got me into the most trouble, it wasn't until I changed schools after putting a kid in the hospital that I promised not to cause any more harm, even to the bullies. But, Bella and Saylor both missed the black long straight hair that had vibrant orange highlights. I had to change my hair to a dirty brown to keep myself safe.

"Stark," I started. Looking at him in the mirror. He was against my bed, slightly sitting back on the bed.

"Yeah?" He asked.

"Do you remember one of your questions from when we first met?" I wondered, turning around to face him.

"When I asked if you were related to Saylor?" He guessed.

"Yeah,"

"Yes, what does that have to do with anything?"

"Stark, you've met me before," I finally said.

"What do you mean?" He still didn't get it.

I decided that the only way to help him remember was to take off my shirt, revealing my phoenix tattoo and Saylor's favorite black laced bra. He's heard me talk about it before, back before I moved, before I had to turn into Bella. "Stark, it's me, Saylor."

"What?" It seemed like he still didn't understand.

I gave a small laugh, "Stark, it's me, Saylor Martez. Your old girlfriend, I guess…"

"Stop messing with me Bella, you told me you didn't know her."

"Because I am her," I tried saying, he still had disbelief written all over his face. "Stark, you have a sister whom I've met. Her name is Mia and you protect her with your life. Your dad is abusive and isn't around half the time. Stark, I howled before I got on that airplane."

"Babe?" He muttered, his voice cracking.

"Yes," I laughed, relieved to see that he finally recognized me.

"Come here," he held out his arms while I went over in his embrace. "I missed you."

"I missed you too, it's been so hard not telling you." I wrapped my hands around his neck while he had his arms around my waist.

"Why, did you leave?" He asked, looking up at me.

I took a deep breath in, then out, "Stark, what do you see in me?"

"What does this have to do with why you left?"

"It, just does."

"What do you see in yourself first?" He wondered.

"I see a dangerous shy girl; who is also a nerd, quiet, and cute; but can be a test subject." I answered, with a frown. Once the words left my mouth I heard Stark laugh.

"Cute? That's what you think?" He raised an eyebrow, making my insecurities eat me up.

"What do you think?" I wondered, giving a slight cough to keep the tears down.

"Baby," he said softly. "To me, you're not just cute. You're pretty, beautiful, babe, you're the gorgeouest girl I know."

"You only disagreed with me because I'm more than cute?" I hinted, soon adding. "Did you just make up that word?"

"Yes babe, I did." He laughed tilting his head, he soon studied me. "Why did you call yourself dangerous and a test subject?"

"Stark, you've only known me since our freshman year." I started, "I'm dangerous. I did something back in 5th grade because someone made fun of my orange eyes."

"It doesn't matter what happened in the past, it's now that matter's isn't it?" Stark tried to comfort me. The Saylor side of me snorted, like he knew.

"It does to me. Since I was born I've been dangerous." I sighed. "I went on that plane because my parents died making sure that my sisters and I wouldn't get used as a test subject. My family and I are different, my brother and I are different. The twins aren't like us, then again they were adopted. But, that still doesn't mean that we don't know if Taylor is like us or not!"

"Okay, okay. Everyone is different babe." Again, like before, he didn't understand.

"Stark, my brother and I have these powers. We can hear through walls, through floors. Andrew could hear us if he wanted to. For all I know he's blocking our voices and keeping Taylor occupied." I closed my eyes, taking a deep breath in then out. "In 5th grade, I got expelled. In 5th grade I sent someone to the hospital. I got into fights before that too because of my eyes. But, they never got that bad… After that I went to a different school, my parents made me promise to never use my powers again. So, as I'd walked past kids who would make fun of my eyes, I had to fight the urge to fight them."

"Sooo, you can hear what the people next door are saying?" Stark asked, beginning to understand the situation.

"Yes, they're arguing over who can have the last chip bad." I answered, with a smile.

He smiled back, then his face faded, "you didn't want to answer that question earlier because you knew what you were going to hear."

I gave a small smile, being happy about him understanding everything. "Yes, but it was because it was also hard to breathe as well."

"Are you ok baby?" He wondered, he was worried about me, a lot. But I didn't blame him, I always kept myself private when it came to my family.

"I just miss my parents, and the twins," I whispered, my lip trembling.

"Oh, sweetie," he frowned, rearranging me so that I was sitting in his lap, to where it seemed like I was in a cradle position. He wrapped his arms even tighter around my hips while I nestled my head into his neck.

"Would you say there's a difference between Saylor and Bella?" I asked, wondering what his answer would be now that he found out about me being Saylor.

"There's some differences but both personalities are beautiful and make you, you."

I gave a small laugh, "what Saylor looked like made Bella have more insecurities than Saylor."

"Yea? They both seem pretty beautiful to me," he rubbed my back, reminding me that I still had my shirt off.

"Bella still wishes she looked like Saylor again. However, the only change was the hair. But Bella changed Saylor a lot. Sometimes I'll get a mix of Bella and Saylor both. Or I'll get a bit of Saylor too," I leaned back some, putting my arms around his neck.

"Hmm, interesting…" He smiled, rubbing my skin. I rearranged myself so I ad one leg on one side of him and my other leg on the other side of him. I sat up while he loosened his grip on my hips.

"Yea?" I smiled, teasingly.

"Yeah." He nodded, pulling me closer to him until our lips locked. We kissed over and over until I leaned away laughing. "What?"

"I never knew this would feel so good, it's our first ever kiss since we've been together," I smiled.

"You're a really good kisser, and it is, isn't?" He smiled back, squeezing me.

"Hm, that would have to be the Saylor part," I squinted my eyes thinking about it.

"It's not. It's the mix of Saylor and Bella. Cause that is still you, and I will love them both. Cause I love you," he said.

"Man, it's been a good minute since I've heard those words from you." I smiled, feeling water in my eyes.

"I know, and I'm so happy I could say them to both you and Saylor." He beamed, pulling me into another kiss.

"I'm gonna give myself the credit for being a good kisser, but I'm gonna say that I love how you always smell good. Especially when you smell like peppermints." I told him.

He rearranged us, picking me up, and crawling to the corner of my bed against the wall and had me in his lap so that I was leaning my back on his chest.

"Peppermints?" He wondered.

"You're the only person I can breathe around other than my house. My reason for leaving school early. It's hard to breathe, almost like a claustrophobic feeling." I explained.

"Ahw," he muttered, understandingly.

"Hey, what are we?" I tilted my head so I could look up at him.

"I don't know, why do you ask?" He sighed after thinking about it.

"I told Taylor you were my boyfriend," I answered, feeling the blush cross my face.

"Really?" He gave a small laugh. "What do you want us to be?"

"I don't know. What we had before I left, we didn't really have a label, almost like a fling or situationship."

"Well, what do you want now?"

"Why are you asking me?!" I was starting to get overwhelmed.

"Because you're the one who mentioned it!" He started to raise his voice, thankfully I hadn't flinched.

"Well, I guess we can officially be boyfriend and girlfriend." I finally said playing with his hand.

"You guess?" He was calmer, and stopped me from playing with his hand and put mine between his.

I was hesitant, everyone I loved seemed to go out of my life. I'm still lucky my brother hasn't left and the fact that I was able to reconnect with Stark.

"Babe?" He was serious now, and I was scared. I didn't say anything, instead I was thinking of the possibilities of this going wrong. I also felt limp, I was breathing slowly. My arms went down as my hand nearly slipped out of Stark's. My body turned off, and fell weightlessly against Stark.

"Bella?" He was a little bit less serious, with a hint of worry.

"You don't understand." I finally said, but with a whisper.

"You're right, I don't understand. But I'd like to try. And I can't do that unless you explain." After the words left his mouth he rearranged us for the third time.

He easily rested me on my bed. My head on my pillows and my body flat on my back, my legs were extended out near the end of the bed. He had both his legs on one side of me, and the other on the side that was closer to the wall. He had both hands on opposite sides of me and he was hovering over me. He leaned in to kiss me, then put his head on my shoulders and then went back to hovering over me.

"It's hard," I whispered again, my voice cracking and feeling the tears roll down my face.

"I know, nobody said that love was easy, did they?" He took one of his hands and raised away the tears.

I finally got the strength to rearrange myself to where I curled myself in a ball, which made Stark rearrange himself as well. He decided to sit with his knees ip and his arms around them, waiting patiently to hear my side.

CHAPTER

1

Stark:

"Everyone I love always seems to leave me or get taken away from me. I'm still lucky that my brother and his family are still with me, along with getting you back in my life." She explained.

I looked at her, curled in a ball, holding herself close like she was scared of every little thing. She still had her shirt on the floor with her other stuff. But I could care less about what she was wearing and more about how she was doing mentally, physically, and emotionally.

"I'm not going anywhere, and I'm never going to leave your side. Even if you transfer across the world, I'll find you again." I promised, this would be semi easy. I already lost her once, and I wasn't going to let that happen for a second time.

"I don't like promises or that promise you just said. We still have several years to live. If I ever make it for a few years," she muttered the last part.

"You will, and I'm gonna make sure of it." I put my hand on her arm, which made her relax a little bit.

"I knew this was gonna go wrong," she sighed.

I gave a small laugh in response and moved myself closer to her, much closer. I unfolded the ball of my dear Peppermint, I extended her legs out and wrapped my own around her hips, and pulled her close to me. I put my arms around her, holding her tightly. I started to give a trail of soft, passionate kisses starting from her jaw line, down to her neck, and then her shoulder.

Once I got a little bit past her shoulder to the start of her arm, I kept my lips there. After a few seconds I felt her head move and placed her beautiful eyes on me. I opened my eyes, not taking my lips off of her and looked up at her. As I thought, she was looking down at me. I smiled and finally took my lips off of her bare skin.

"Peppermints?" I wondered, making a small smile appear on her pretty face.

"You're gonna love that word now," she rolled her eyes, escaping a laugh. Ohh yes I am.

"New favorite word," I told her. Soon adding, "Actually, I'm thinking about putting that on the collection of nicknames for my girlfriend."

"Collection?!" Her eyes went big as I gave a small chuckle.

"Yup, we've got: Babe, Baby, Saylor which is in my favorites category, and Peppermints, which is also in my favorites category as well." I smiled.

"Don't use Saylor in public, it could put my life even more on the line," she explained.

"I won't," I nodded. I took my hand, with my pointer finger I slid it down the middle of her back. Watching as the goosebumps traveled all over her arms and back. "And I'll love the goosebumps I give you."

Before she had time to scowl at me, Andrew yelled, "dinner!"

We both acted fast, we quickly got off the bed and I threw her the shirt she was wearing earlier. She got it on and we almost left the room before I stopped and grabbed her arm.

"What?" She looked back at me, I answered by pulling her in for a kiss. She pulled away after a minute or two and said, "Let's go before my brother finds something to embarrass me. I'm sure he's already coming up with something."

"Then why not stay up here a little longer?" I teased.

"Come on!" She rolled her eyes and took my hand pulling me through the house and down the stairs to the dining room; which passed the small-ish, big kitchen.

After coming down the stairs and instead of going through the living room there was a small hallway that led to the kitchen's bar or island area, the dining room, and on the opposite side, a bathroom and an office.

When we reached the dining room Mrs. Sabrina, Mr. Andrew, cute Taylor, and an older man were already sitting down eating.

"Hello Stark, nice seeing you today," Mr. Andrew smiled over at me.

"You too," I smiled back, sitting in the chair that Saylor led me to.

"Mr. Leon, I didn't know you were here." Saylor smiled, sitting down next to me and looking over at the older man who I assumed was Mr. Leon.

"Grandpa wanted to visit!" Taylor exclaimed, making it clear that Mr. Leon was Mrs. Sabrina's dad.

"That's cool!" Saylor beamed.

"Starky, are you spending the night? Auntie Bella said I may not be able to sleep with her tonight." Taylor pouted looking over at me.

"Oh, did she now?" I gave a small laugh, looking between Taylor and my Peppermint.

"Mhm, she said that daddy wanted her to do something big and she didn't know what the outcome would be." Taylor explained.

"I see…" I nodded, finally understanding. I looked around the room: Mr. Leon, Mrs. Sabrina, and Mr. Andrew was talking. I was certain that Mr. Andrew was also paying attention to both me and them. Saylor was eating quietly, looking down at her food. Lastly, Taylor was waiting to see if I'd be spending the night or not. I'm sure that either way she would be happy one way or another.

"Starky, are you spending the night or not?" Taylor whined asking again.

"Pumpkin, be patient," Saylor looked up from her food and over to Taylor.

"It's fine," I reassured. To me, it looked like Saylor wasn't too okay, and I knew I had to get to the bottom of it. "Yes Taylor, I'll be spending the night; but I need to get some stuff from my house first."

"Yay!" Taylor beamed.

"If you'd like I could bring you there, I do have a small errand to do," Mr. Andrew offered, which made Saylor scowl at him.

"It's fine, thank you," I politely declined.

"Okay," Mr. Andrew smiled.

"Starky, can I show you my stuffed animal collection when you come back from your home?" Taylor wondered.

"Pumpkin," Saylor began to say.

"Babe, it's ok." I looked over at her, she seemed a little frustrated and off than she usually was. Was she okay? Is she jealous of Taylor enjoying my company? Doesn't she know that I'd give up my life for her?

"Sorry," Taylor mumbled.

"You're fine, but maybe. Alright?" I turned my attention back to Taylor as I placed my hand I wasn't eating with on Saylor's knee, rubbing my thumb along it.

"Mhm!" Taylor perked right back up, making me smile.

The rest of the dinner wasn't that bad. Saylor stayed quiet as can be in between questions that Mr. Leon was asking.

"Any plans for college kids?"

"I haven't had the chance to think about it, I might take a gap year." I shrugged.

"I might lay low and do online college," Saylor whispered quietly. At times Mr. Andrew or I would have to repeat what she said, or she would speak up herself. Mr. Leon would also turn to Mr. Andrew and Mrs. Sabrina to ask questions as well.

"You're fine with this boy sleeping with your sister?"

"I'm a chill free kind of guy sir. Plus, I remember my 17 years. Also, Stark is a good kid," Mr. Andrew answered, smiling my way. Mr. Leon then turned to his daughter.

"We're perfectly okay with it. Bella has been through a lot and I don't want to be the person she hates. Plus, we trust both of the kids to learn from their actions and they're almost adults. I'm also not even related ro her, only by sister-in-law. If Andrew is okay with it, then I'm fine with it as well."

"If Taylor got a boyfriend at 17 or 16 and he was able to spend the night, would you have him spend the night in her bed with her?" Mr. Leon quizzed.

"Please sir, I don't want to think about that right now. Please understand that Bella is my sister, not my daughter." Mr. Andrew seemed a little upset by this conversation.

"Don't different adults, guardians, or families teach or parent kids in different ways? Not everyone has the same rule system." I wondered, accusatory. Which all of that was true. I knew it was. Saylor had some bad stuff and I did as well. In fact I still am going through it. Mr. Leon looked at me long and hard, like I created a whole other problem.

"I suppose you're right boy," Mr. Leon mumbled, ending the conversation. Mr. Andrew and Saylor looked at me a little surprised and happy.

When dinner was over I decided to leave and pick stuff up from my house along with taking a shower. Once I got to my house I was surprised to see my younger sister outside on the porch steps.

"You're gonna catch a cold being out here wearing that Mia," I informed her when I sat down next to her. She was wearing barely any clothes; athletic black short shorts, and a spaghetti strapped crop top. "What are you even doing out here anyways?"

"Dad's inside yelling at mom," she whispered.

"I swear, they should divorce already," I grumbled standing up and picking up my 12 year old sister.

"I don't understand why you still carry me. I'm too old to be carried." Mia glared her hazel nut eyes, which we both shared with our mom, at me.

"Bella hates it when I carry her too. But, I love carrying my two favorite girls," I smiled and opened the front door. I could already hear my dad screaming as I walked in, thankfully my room and bathroom was right next to the front door.

"You have a lot of favorites," Mia crossed her arms as I put her down in my room.

"I'm gonna be in the shower, pack me a bag so I can spend the night at Bella's." I told her, ignoring what she said.

"You're gonna leave me! With mom and dad arguing?! I'm really gonna get a cold!" She growled.

"Yes, Bella has me worried and she told me something really important, and she really needs me. Stay in my room if you want, sneak around mom and dad." I explained.

"Okay, I'll pack a bag for you. Take care of Bella and tell her and Taylor I say hi." She sighed, knowing that Bella was always my weakness especially when I was worried about her.

"Thank you," I smiled and headed into my bathroom.

"Saylor, tell me something," I was back at Saylor's in her room. She was cleaning up her room a little bit, she seemed like she was stressed cleaning. I was against her bed watching her skeptically, trying to figure out what was wrong.

"What do you want me to tell you?!" She cried out looking over at me, stopping what she was doing.

"Come here peppermint," I held my arms out, wanting to hug her, hold her, and never wanting to let her go. She dropped her clothes and walked over, tears forming. Other than today, I've never seen her cry, let alone seeing Saylor cry.

"I... I'm gonna mess this up," she mumbled.

"I'm not going anywhere," I wrapped my arms around her, pulling her to me. I had her comfortable on my lap so that he was able to put her head on my chest.

"One way or another you will," she said with no emotion.

"But, I'll always come back," I squeezed her, wanting her to believe me.

"Fine," it sounded like she didn't believe me, but I could tell that she no longer wanted to argue it. I took my hand and moved it to her back, having my hand go under her shirt. Doing the same thing as earlier, I took my pointer finger and slid it down her back. Once again, I watched the goosebumps travel.

"Peppermint, your kisses and seeing goosebumps created by me are now my favorite things thanks to you," I smiled at her.

"I'd rather have you kiss me then the goosebumps," she glared up at me.

"Oh yea?" I teased, rearranging her. One knee on one side of me and her other on the other side of me. As I attempted to get this settled, Saylor laughed and helped me out. She sat up and I put my hands on her waist as she put her hands at the back of my neck.

It was only a second later when we started making out, her hands were roaming through my hair, getting tugged every so often, making it a tad bit difficult to breathe. I had my own hands on her hips guiding them up, down, forward, and back, applying bits of pressure making it so she would also grumble as our lips would part, but would always find their way back to each other.

After a while, I realized that I had something to ask her about, "hey babe." I stopped my hands, pulled away, and looked at her.

"What's wrong?" She asked, leaning back, her hands relaxing and resting on my neck.

"Are you jealous about your niece having a slight crush on me?" I wondered.

She closed her eyes, taking a deep breath in. As she let it out she answered, still with her eyes closed, "yes, I don't know why, but yes, I am."

"I'm going to tell you the truth, Taylor's a cute girl, but there's only room for three girls in my life plus my heart. Those people are; my mom, my sister, and my Saylor. Don't feel jealous babe," I explained, making her smile.

"Thanks for the reassurance," after she said those words, her warm, electrifying, soft lips came back to mine.

When she pulled apart she planted a kiss on my forehead, then on my cheek, and lastly my neck. "I should get in the shower. You can visit Taylor's room and she can show you her stuffed animal collection."

"You're gonna be ok, right?" I asked.

"Yes, I'm going to be okay," she laughed a little and got out of my lap.

"Hey, I gotta be sure," I laughed too with a shrug.

Bella/Saylor:

"But, good." Stark nodded getting off my bed. He then walked over to me, gave me a kiss on the forehead and headed out of my room.

I smiled with a sigh of relief and then grabbed an oversized t-shirt Andrew gave me along with underwear. After, I headed to my bathroom which was right across from my bedroom, closed the door and took off my shirt and stared at myself for a minute.

Thinking:

What were the odds of Stark also moving schools? Let alone the same one I went to. I only decided to help him that one day at school because I wanted to make sure it was Stark, that and he looked like he had no idea where to go, which I found funny. I wasn't too surprised when he became friends with Landon, he was stereotyped to be the "football player" and "popular boy" at school. But even when Landon and his friends talked bad about me, Stark always defended me, even if that got him to be teased. I later found out that when he found me in Sasha's nurse office with a bloody nose, it was because of me. It was wrong, it made me angry. I found out through text, Andrew had to make me "babysit" Taylor to keep my calm down. I hated it when people got hurt because of me, it wasn't right.

My thinking soon got interrupted when I heard a knock at the door, which was probably best. I didn't want to go down a spiral and end up crying or getting angry again.

"Yes?" I looked towards the door, recognizing the breathing on the other side.

"How are you feeling?" Andrew opened the door, coming in, and shutting it behind him.

"I'm a lot better, I'm glad that I was able to tell him everything." I answered

"Good." Andrew nodded.

"Andrew," I started. "Does Sabrina know about our family?"

"Yea, she's known since the first time we attempted to make out. She smiled and said that my hearing would come in handy. She also said that it makes sense as to why my lips were always warm." Andrew explained, smiling the whole time.

"Oh my gosh!" I rolled my eyes, lightly punching his shoulder.

"Hey, I don't blame you. I still remember when Sabrina and I were 17," Andrew took a step back, hands in the air like he was surrendering.

"Go away! Let me shower!" I opened the bathroom door and pushed him out. "Plus, you're still in that phase!"

By the time I closed the door, Andrew was laughing. I rolled my eyes again, glancing at myself in the mirror. My cheeks filled with blush, this time I laughed and got ready to shower.

"This is Dolly, she's my favorite and my precious. Just like Auntie Bella is your precious," I heard Taylor explain to Stark. I was done in the shower and was walking to Taylor's room where I heard Taylor and Stark.

"Really?!" Stark sounded surprised, "where did you get that from?"

"Mhm! And daddy told me." She nodded, by this time I was in her doorway. Stark was facing away from the door and Taylor was facing the door. I smiled and put my finger to my lips when Taylor saw me. Hoping that she'd understand that I wanted to surprise Stark.

"What's this one's name?" I saw Stark hold up a gray medium sized elephant.

"Her name is Ellie!" Taylor beamed, I got as close as I could to Stark and sat down. I put my arms around his shoulders and kissed the side of his neck.

"Hey," I whispered.

"Hey Peppermint," Stark slid his hands up and down my arms, planting a kiss on my wrists.

"You guys are cute together," Taylor complimented. Before Stark or I could answer we heard Andrew from the doorway.

"They are, aren't they?" Andrew came in and sat on Taylor's bed.

"Daddy!!" Taylor got up and ran to her father's lap.

"Hey sweetie," Andrew laughed, fixing her on his lap.

"Is it time for bed?" Taylor looked up at him.

"Yep, it's time to get ready for bed. Your mom is getting ready to leave." Andrew answered, taking her off his lap.

"Oh-kay," Taylor sighed, going over to get her pj's and running out of her room towards Sabrina.

"Thanks for letting me stay the night," Stark thanked.

"Of course, keep her safe for me alright?" Andrew smiled at us. We were now standing up.

"Yes sir." Stark confirmed.

"Good night Saylor. Good night Stark." Andrew turned to me then Stark.

"Night," I mumbled.

"Good night," Stark nodded, Andrew smiled one more time then left the room.

"Come on, let's go to my room." I grabbed Stark's hand and pulled him to my room.

Once I got my door closed Stark grabbed my hand and pulled me to him. He put his arms around my waist and put his soft lips on mine. I grabbed the collar of his shirt and deepened the kiss, walking backwards blindly to my bed. When I got to my bed Stark lifted me up on the bed, we kept going backwards, still kissing. Our lips would separate for a second or two then found their way back to each other. At one point I felt Stark's hand go under my shirt at my waist. After a minute or two I pulled away, my eyes fluttering open along with Stark's.

"Not now, not tonight?" He guessed, making me smile. I gave him a gentle kiss on his lips and put my thumb on his bottom lip.

"I love you," I whispered smiling, as I felt the tears come out of my eyes.

"I love you too Peppermint," he took his hand that wasn't touching my bare skin and removed my own hand off his lip and kissed my knuckles. "Come on, let's lay down."

So that's what we did. We laid down on my bed, Stark close to the wall, his arms around me, facing my mirror. I was facing him, snuggled up next to him, my hands on his chest.

"Hang on," Stark sat up.

"What?" I wondered, propping myself up with my elbow.

"I wanna be ready to go to sleep," he took off his shirt and threw it by his bag and laid back down. I unpropped my elbow and snuggled back into Stark.

"How are you?" I asked, looking up at him.

"I'm good, you?" He answered, asking it back to me.

"A lot better," I smiled.

"Do you plan to go back to school tomorrow?" He questioned, moving a strand of hair out of my eyes.

"I don't think so," I shook my head. "Are you?"

"No," he rearranged us to where I was on my back and he was on his stomach, burying his head against my neck and kissing it.

"What about your parents?"

"Dad doesn't care what I do, and mom's too busy worrying about Mia. They both don't really care what I do." Stark sighed, resting his head on my shoulders.

"At least you have some people who care about you," I told him as I ran my fingers through his dark brown short-long floppy hair. His response was to grunt and wrap his arms around my waist, pulling me closer to him as much as he could.

"Sleep," he mumbled after giving my shoulder a kiss and resting his head back on my shoulder.

"Alright sleepy head, good night." I laughed, attempting to kiss his forehead.

"Good night babe," and with that he was fast asleep. I smiled and closed my eyes, going to sleep.

CHAPTER

2

Stark:

My three most important girls were all different pieces of fragile glass.

One was able to break so easily, that one was my mom. Everytime my dad and her argue she'd lock herself in the bathroom, with Mia in her room, or with me in my room. She'd break down and think about how she could love someone who always dismisses her. I always try to convince her to divorce my dad, but she's always too scared. It's pointless when he comes because he'll be getting up and leaving again. Or he leaves for a year and when he gets back it's only 2 months which is already hell. When he comes back he usually comes back angry and is yelling at everyone and arguing. It was rare when he'd ask how we're doing.

But, the second piece is strong, but not as strong as the other one. However, they are stubborn, this piece would be Mia. She tries to act strong and she hates crying. When our parents argue she stays away and usually goes outside, my room, or her own room. She barely eats when my dad is around. She's really smart and fun to be around, but she's very stubborn and gets mad at herself for crying. Which is really upsetting, because it's natural to cry, especially when it comes to my dad.

Now, the last piece, this one is so strong, she makes me feel like I don't deserve her. Maybe I knew her for a while now, but I've never met someone like her. This one is my Peppermint, my Saylor, my Bella. People may make fun of her but she's more than just someone to judge just because she answers all the questions right. Or because she has orange eyes, or is even quiet. I'm not just saying this because I'm her boyfriend. I'm saying this because it's true. People judge people the same way they judge a book by it's cover.

I still remember the first day of school here, I was completely lost and I remember, my Saylor was talking to me in a quiet voice, helping me. She was the first girl and person who was that kind to me. I also remember going to my mom and sister, and I told them that I was going to marry her. I still remember Mia asking what about Saylor. Thank goodness they were the same person, in a sense...

I always think about the first time I met Saylor and Bella both. Even now as I watch her sleeping carefully. She was against me, her hands folded and to her chest, facing me. Her lips a little parted, she looked so delicate. At some point last night I heard someone come in here and turned off Saylor's alarm. It was now 8am, we would be at school by now. My phone was going off, but I didn't care, I just left it be. I was afraid of waking Saylor up if I were to move, after all I did have one arm around her waist and the other free, placing wherever was comfortable.

"Mmm," Saylor started to move around. It was now 10:30am and I stayed in bed the whole time, Saylor in my arms.

"Are you waking up now baby?" I asked this just as her eyelids fluttered open.

"Mmm," she repeated, stretching her arms over her head, a smile crossing her beautiful face.

"I don't know if that's a yes or not," I gave a small laugh, planting a kiss on her forehead.

"It's a, I'm awake but I want to stay in bed," she answered, cupping my ace with her hands and giving me a kiss.

"How'd you sleep?" I wondered.

"Pretty good, you?" She replied with.

"I slept good as well," I leaned in and gave her a kiss. When I pulled away, Saylor's arms were still around my neck and was pulling me in for more. "Baby, I love you, but not now."

"Not a fan of morning breath?" She laughed.

"Not really," I let out a laugh as well.

"Alright, well, we have the day off to do whatever we want, so let's get ready." She lightly pushed me to my side, so that she was able to get out of bed. She walked up to her mirror and lifted her hair, "ugh, my hair is a mess."

"Do you know how beautiful you look right now?" I questioned, she looked behind her, at me, with squinting eyes.

"You're only saying that because all I'm wearing is an oversized t-shirt on top of my undies. Including the fact that you have a good view of my legs," she explained.

"You know, I'm not that dirty minded and I'm not that much of a perv. I love your kisses and I love kissing you. But, I'm not about getting your clothes off until we take that step. And, I don't know about you, but I don't plan on taking that step any time soon." I sighed, explaining my thoughts. Somehow this made Saylor smile, she came over to me and gave me a kiss on the forehead.

"That is one of my favorite parts about you," she then turned and went back to grab her clothes. I rolled on my back and put my arm on top of my face.

"I have the world's hottest and bestest girlfriend ever," I mumbled, knowing that she could hear me.

"I don't think bestest is a word," she laughed. I moved my arm and glanced at her, watching her struggle to put on jeans, her foot kept on wanting to go in one of the rips on her jeans.

"Doesn't matter," I got out of bed and walked to my bag, grabbing my clothes for the day.

"Good morning, how'd you sleep?" Mr. Andrew greeted Saylor and I as we walked into the kitchen.

"Morning, and I slept good," Saylor smiled, turning to me she asked. "Cereal? We don't have much breakfast stuff."

"Sure," I answered and looked back to Mr. Andrew. "I slept good too."

"Good," Mr. Andrew smiled, then turned toward Saylor who put our bowls down where we sat last night. "Taylor was upset again this morning."

"I'll find a way to make it up to her, maybe I'll take her on a shopping spree or something," Saylor sighed, turning towards me. We were both now sitting down, "I usually wake Taylor up in the mornings. I didn't wake her up yesterday and since I slept in today, I didn't wake her up this morning."

"I see," I nodded, understanding. "What do you do differently than what they do? She's gotta have a reason why she gets upset when you don't wake her up."

"Saylor and Taylor have a special connection with each other and Taylor is also attached to Saylor. Plus Saylor spoils the little girl." Mr. Andrew explained.

"So little Taylor got herself a cool aunt?" I guessed, smiling at Saylor whose cheeks were pink.

"Yep," Mr. Andrew smiled. "I'm pretty sure I heard a phone going off this morning."

"Yea, that was me." I nodded.

"Did you check to see who it was?" Saylor wondered.

"No, but it's probably Landon asking where I am. No biggie," I answered.

"Well, glad you guys are awake. I'll be in the office for a while until I have to get Taylor. See you kids later." Mr. Andrew got up and walked in the direction of the office.

"So, what do you want to do today?" I looked over at Saylor who just finished eating.

"Watch movies and snuggle on the couch?" She suggested.

"Sounds good." So that was what we did the whole time. When Taylor got home she joined us too. I never checked my phone while we were watching movies and Saylor promised a shopping spree at the mall with Taylor.

When I arrived home Landon's car was there and he was sitting on the porch steps.

"Hey man," I greeted when I got to him.

"Hey, why didn't you answer any of my texts?" He asked.

"Oh, I was busy," I shrugged as I opened the front door to find my dad standing in the living room, arms crossed. My mom was sitting on the couch in tears and I saw Mia in tears as well, though she was on the floor in the corner, her cheek looking a little pink.

"Why weren't you at school today?! Where were you?!" My dad started yelling.

"Why do you care?" I asked calmly, not leaving my eyes off of Mia.

"Stark, please answer the question," my mom spoke up.

"Fine, but tell me what happened to Mia first." I crossed my arms and squinted my eyes at my dad.

"She wasn't behaving the way I raised her, so I taught her a lesson." My dad answered.

"Oh? The last time I checked you didn't even raise her. It was me and mom who did all that." I laughed.

"Where were you?!" My dad barked.

"With my girlfriend!" I yelled back.

"Bro, since when are you leaving me out of the loop? Since when did you have a girlfriend?" I heard Landon from behind me. I wish he didn't follow me inside, then again, I don't know how much he heard while he was outside.

"Good question Landon. When did you get a girlfriend of yours?" My dad softened a little.

I sighed and looked over at Landon, "yea, and I'm sorry. I didn't tell you because we didn't want rumors." I looked over at my dad. "Why does this concern you? You don't even care about us."

"Well, I am your father. Some things do concern me," my dad stopped yelling.

"I started going out with a girl since I came to the school and then we finally put a label on it last night. Lastly, my girlfriend's name is Bella." I explained.

"Wait, Bella Larren? The weird girl with orange eyes and is quiet and is a huge nerd?" Landon clarified. "The girl who came a little before you did?"

"Landon, do you know anything else of this Bella?" My father looked over at Landon.

"Some girls say she has a tattoo on her chest," Landon shrugged.

"Stark, my boy, why don't you invite Bella over for dinner?" My father smiled, looking back at me.

"Maybe in a few months," I told him and looked over at Mia. "Sis, go do what I told you to do last night and for you too."

"Okay," Mia got up and ran up to her room on the second floor.

"Landon, go home, we can hang out at your house tomorrow. I promise," I then turned to Landon.

"Fine, see you later man," Landon shook his head disappointingly and walked out the door. I felt a little bad, but I had to get Mia and I out of the house. I looked over at my dad just as I saw Mia go into my room.

"If you're gonna want to be in my life and know the people I hang out with, then be a better dad and husband. Other than that you are nothing like a father to me," I glared at him before glancing to my mom. "I'm if I made you worry, I love you a lot."

"I love you too Stark," her lips trembling, holding her hands together to her chest.

"Are you ready?" I asked Mia as she came to my side.

"Yeah," she nodded.

"Go say goodbye to mom and then we'll leave," I ordered. She ran over to our mom, gave her a hug and a kiss on the cheek. My mom whispered something in her ear and then she came back to me.

"Ready," she whispered.

With that we left without a word, and when we got to the car I decided to call Saylor, and put her on speaker so it was easier to drive.

"Hello?" She answered.

"Hey babe, up for another night?" I wondered.

"Um, sure. Just hang on," she said. "Andrew! Stark's spending another night!"

"Got it!" Mr. Andrew yelled back.

"Oh, and Mia's gonna be there too," I added.

"Sounds good!" I could feel her smile through the phone.

"Alright, love you," I smiled.

"Love you, see you soon," she hung up in a chirpy tone.

I looked over at Mia who was staring out her window.

"How are you sis?" I asked, concerned.

"I'm alright, you?" She looked up at me.

"I'm doing good, glad that I was able to get you out of there."

Bella/Saylor:

I decided to shower before Stark came, plus it sounded like he was driving as well. After my shower I got dressed, went back into my regular clothes and cleaned up my room. While I was getting dressed I learned that putting jeans on after you shower is more difficult than when you don't shower and put jeans on. It also didn't help that my jeans had holes in them so my foot kept getting stuck.

Anyways, I figured that my room would still be a little bit messy when Stark and Mia showed up, but I ended up finishing and had time to do whatever I wanted. I decided to flop on my bed and play Cats & Soup. It only lasted 15 minutes when I heard the doorbell ring.

"Saylor, your guests are here." Andrew said from his office.

"I know, I'm getting it," I told him, going out of my room and working my way down the stairs. "Hey guys," I greeted when I opened the door.

"Hi Bella," Mia waved.

"Come on in," I opened the door wider so that they could come in. "Taylor's at the park with Sabrina right now"

"Why don't we put our stuff down and then we can take a walk to the park?" Stark suggested, putting their stuff by the stairs.

"Sure, just let me grab my shoes," I smiled running up to my room.

Once I got my shoes we headed out the door. Mia stayed with us for a while until I told her we would be going straight for a while where she started skipping ahead. This gave me the opportunity to ask Stark what took so long.

"What took you so long to arrive at my house? It sounded like you were driving." I wondered. We were holding hands, but I was hugging onto his arm, our bodies close to each other.

"Worrying about me Peppermint?" Stark teased.

"Yes, I was able to shower and finish cleaning my room. We both knew how bad it was when you left," I explained with a nod.

"Well, I had to do a 'pick-me-up' for Mia," he sighed.

Even if he was fine, I was still concerned about Stark, "Stark, are you ok?"

"I... I don't want to talk about it here. But I've got it handled," he looked down at me with a sad small smile and squeezed my hand.

"All the people who say they have it handled turn into a complete mess and still don't want help until last minute." I said sternly, knowingly because I've had the experience with this. I also didn't want Stark to go through it as well.

"Well, I'll be telling you when we get to your house," he told me. I had to support his decision on not wanting to share now, even though I knew it would bother me until he shared.

"To the right Mia," I instructed.

"What happened?" I asked as soon as I closed the door to my room. We were back home, Mia and Taylor were in the backyard jumping on the trampoline.

"First things first," Stark smiled, grabbing me by the waist and pulling me in for a kiss. I let him have two kisses before I pulled away and put my finger on his lips. This made him sigh, he took my wrist and took my fingers off his lips.

"Tell me Stark. I love you and care about you," I told him and put my hands on his chest, his hands were back on my waist, which I was okay with.

"My dad isn't so good. He leaves my mom in pain, leaves Mia starving, and leaves me mad. He barely comes and sees us and when he does he's arguing with my mom and Mia never eats that much when he's around. He barely even acts like a father and I am giving him one more chance to prove to me that he is a father. Plus, he pays too much attention to his secret work. I also want my mom to divorce him." He explained, taking breaths in between.

I had no words, all I did was look into his eyes and know that he was saying the truth. I didn't even have to think twice to know that what he was saying was true, I already knew, I felt it. It was hard to read his expression. My mind was racing, trying to figure out how to make him smile again.

When a thought came in, one I was willing to do, I gave a small smile and gave a small shove, making Stark go against my bed. I took off my shirt, dropped it to the floor, and walked over to him putting my hands on his chest. I leaned in and kissed him; lightly rubbing the top of my teeth on the bottom of his lip when I pulled away.

Automatically, Stark put his hands on my hips, pulling me in for more kisses. I slid my hands down to the bottom of his shirt and took it off of him, throwing it over my shoulder to the floor with my own. Stark moved me to where I was against the bed, put me on my back against the bed. He had his hands on my sides, under my armpits; slowly moving them down as his lips made a trail starting at my lips, down to my neck, to my chest, my stomach, and then he lifted his head once he got to my waist where my jeans button and zipper was.

"May I?" He wondered.

"Yes, just the button." I answered, with a mutter.

"Yes ma'am," he nodded, listening. When he kissed me there, more pressure was applied. I had no choice but to close my eyes and let a sigh of pleasure escape.

A while passed and we were both lying down, we still had our shirts off and on the floor. I had my hands on Stark's chest, my fingers making hearts or stars on his skin. Stark's hands were hugging my waist to him, kissing the side of my neck and behind my ears, every so often he'd gently bite my ear. When he was done he held me tight and buried his face into my neck.

"How are you?" I asked. "Are you doing better?"

"I'm doing a lot better. Still a little upset, but you're a good distraction," he mumbled, his warm breath against my skin.

"Good, I'm glad," I smiled.

"What are the girls doing?" He wondered.

"Watching a movie and eating popcorn," I answered.

"What are they watching?"

"Aladin."

"What about your brother?"

"He's cleaning up the kitchen and making dinner with Sabrina."

"Do you know what time it is?"

I slid my eyes to the clock, "6:30."

"When did we get back to the house? Do you remember or know?"

I closed my eyes, thinking, "5pm."

This made him shift and move his head to look at me, eyes wide, "one hour and a half ago?!"

"Mhm," I nodded.

"Dang," he said, burying his face back into my neck.

"Andrew suspects it. But doesn't do anything about it."

"Remember that he's your brother, he may be your guardian but it's not like he's your parent. Plus, didn't he tell Mr. Leon that he remembers his teenage years?"

"I know he's my brother, but yet, you still call him Mr. Andrew instead of just Andrew." I laughed, soon adding, "and yes, I remember, and he keeps telling me that. But.."

"One, it's more polite to say Mr. Andrew. And two, you want him to keep thinking you're a virgin?"

I didn't know how I felt about what he said, but I knew having two topics at once was difficult for me.

"Stark." I took my hands and pushed up on his shoulder so that we could look at each other.

"Yes?"

"He's my brother, you don't have to add a Mr. in front of it. It's ok to call him Andrew."

"Alright, I'll call him Andrew from now on."

"Okay, and I am a virgin." I said the last part seriously.

"I know, and what I said this morning still applies," he nodded. This made me laugh.

"Sure," I teased with a smile, this time he laughed.

"At least what I said with the bestest girlfriend is absolutely true," he said as he leaned to give me a kiss on the cheek, the forehead, and then lastly the lips.

"Dinner's just about ready. We should grab our shirts and put them back on," I told Stark when our lips parted.

"Darn, I was just about to kiss you some more," Stark teased as he worked his way off the bed. I rolled my eyes smiling as I sat up to put on my shit that Stark threw at me.

CHAPTER

3

Stark:

Distance means so little, when someone means so much. I don't really know who came up with the saying, but I can tell you that it popped in my mind this morning. Today was a Saturday, and I woke up before Saylor again. We were lucky that it was a weekend and we weren't going to skip school again.

That saying popped up as I realized that I promised Landon I'd go see him. Meaning having to leave my Peppermint to go to the mall, where she could be in danger. Although she wasn't going to be alone, she had Taylor going with her.

But being away from her, it was like she took a part of me, and I don't know if I'd get it back. It felt like agony; thinking about her and I being separated made me homesick. A random thought occurred as Saylor moved around against me. It wasn't really random, but what if I proposed to Saylor at the end of the year? A day after graduation, I'd have to find a job and get a lot of money.

Here's the thing though, we actually became official three days ago and I want to marry her. Though I wanted to marry her since I first met Bella. But even before, I always loved Saylor, we just never did anything, which was the beauty of our relationship, it made it all the more innocent. But that never changed the fact that I saw her in my future.

"Man, what am I think?" I sighed, whispering to myself.

"I don't know, what are you thinking?" Saylor yawned, stretching her arms almost hitting my face.

"I didn't know you were awake," I told her as she opened her eyes.

"Mhm," she nodded before saying, "let's go brush our teeth and then get back in bed."

I smiled as she sat up, "can't get enough of my kisses?"

Her response was looking back at me, rolling her eyes with a teasing smile. I smiled back, sat up, and gave her a kiss on her neck, then had to move her sleeve to kiss her shoulder.

"Don't make me put my arms around your neck and lean us back on the bed with my lips on your," she threatened.

"Is that a threat?" I teased.

"It can be," she shot back.

"Alright, let's go brush our teeth," I laughed with an eye roll.

"Then let's brush our teeth! But, do you remember my girls?" She got off the bed and yanked me off too. She pulled me all the way to the bathroom.

"Rachel, Carly, and Lola?" I guessed, remembering when I last saw them at the airport when Saylor got taken from me.

"Yea," she gave a slight smile, pulling a picture out the drawer.

"What's this?" I wondered.

"It's a picture of us before me and you met, it's our freshman year." She gave a small smile and handed me the picture.

It was her and the three crazy ass girls. I was easily able to point out Saylor, her black hair with orange highlights was up in a ponytail. The girls looking like their normal 'bad girl' selves. Saylor was the leader of the group; all of them were wearing black and had enough skin showing that I was certain that every guy wanted to be with them. Though, I don't know how I ended up being with Saylor...

"Wow." Was all I could manage to say, some of the phoenix tattoo was showing. It made me sad, because it was before she had to go into hiding, she was so much happier than she is now.

"Yea, we thought we were going to run the school. We did though, remember? But, that was before I had to leave." She nodded, looking away.

"You miss them, don't you," this wasn't a question in any way.

"I do, I really miss them. If we were at the high school we go to now; hell, Bella would be scared of them. Like I said the other night, Saylor was trouble." She explained, her voice a faint whisper.

"Baby," I frowned, putting the picture down and holding her tightly to my body, hoping to comfort her. As expected she wrapped her arms around my neck and I felt her wet tears on my bare shoulder. I rocked us side to side rubbing my hand against her back.

After a while she leaned back and wiped her eyes, "are you doing better?" I asked.

"Yea, let's brush our teeth," she nodded and cleared her throat.

"Okay," I said, giving her a kiss on the forehead.

"Are you still going to see Landon today?" Mia asked. We were all in the dining room finishing our breakfast.

"Yea, I promised him I would." I answered.

"You're seeing Landon?" Saylor perked up.

"Oh, yea, I am. I forgot to mention it yesterday, but when Mia and I were back at the house and I was yelling at my dad, Landon was there as well. I had to mention you, but I'll make sure he doesn't mention it to anyone at the school." I explained, Saylor and Andrew exchanged glances.

"It's ok, rumors are rumors. I'm okay with going public if you are," she smiled.

"Are you sure?" I wondered, this was a little strange. I know we didn't really talk about being public, let alone at school.

"Yea, I am." She nodded, still smiling.

"Alright, cool." I smiled back at her.

"I'm going to head to the bathroom, I'll be right back." She said, getting up to clear her dish. I wanted to make sure she was gone before I turned to Andrew.

"Um, Andrew, could we go for a little car ride? I want to talk to you about something." I asked, starting to get nervous.

"Sure, wanna go now?" He answered with a smile.

"Yea, sure," I nodded.

"Cool, let's go," Andrew got up, clearing both our plates. I got up following, texting Saylor that I'd be back. When we finally got in the car, Andrew drove a few blocks away, and then soon stopped the car. "What's up kiddo?"

"May I marry your sister?" I asked nervously, already feeling some sweat

"Why?" He wondered.

"Because, I love her. When we're apart, but like far apart, it's like she's taking a part of me away from myself. I don't know if I'll ever get it back. She's got my heart on lock down and it's all hers. She can do whatever she wants with it," I explained.

"Give me more reasons, I know you have them, kid."

"All my life, I've protected everyone I loved. When I met your sister, all I wanted to do was protect her. When I found out she was in danger, all I ever wanted to do was protect her like ever. I'm scared of what's going to happen when she goes to the mall with Taylor, in fact I'm terrified." I took a deep breath and exhaled.

"Keep going,"

"She's the most beautiful girl I've ever seen. She's so kind, smart, and calm. I love her so much! I love the way she acts around kids, I love all the ways I can tease her, and she's an amazing kisser too."

"You're holding one more thing back."

"Before I even realized that she was Saylor, I wanted to marry her. I told my mom and Mia about her. I really want to marry your sister, but I want to have your approval." I smiled, knowing I was red from ear to ear.

"You know, there's a history of the Martez family getting married after high school," Andrew looked out his window, a smile on his face.

"There is?" I questioned.

"Yea, it goes way back," he nodded. Adding, "when one of us Martez family members falls in love and the couple make out a lot; the guys want to purpose by the end of highschool. It's almost like we have soulmates."

"So, Saylor and I are, or could be soulmates?"

"Yes, and I think my daughter is half a Martez. Which is why I'm so protective of her. But I know that she is safe with Saylor."

"Can you tell me more about the family history of the Martezes? At least if there's any more powers or spirituality?" I wandered out of curiosity.

"Sure," he smiled. "As Saylor mentioned, the Martez family is different. We gain powers as we get older, when we are thirty we will have gotten all our powers." He paused and looked over at me.

"Mhm,"

"Right now, Saylor only has the capability of hearing things through walls and floors, along with powerful punches and kicks. The reason why she got that kid in the hospital is because she made it hard for him to breathe; it traumatized her unfortunately, but I guess that happens. She also has her warm breath and will always be warm. She'll never feel baking hot in the hot summers, but she'll feel like a warm fire during the winter. Warm enough that you can snuggle her and not feel like you're sweating."

"Are there any more powers you gain?"

"At 20 you will get new powers, right now I can hear our sisters and Taylor playing music and singing along. Saylor can't hear us, which is why I drove so far. This other power you get is basically when you have a child, this one just comes naturally. The woman get the power when they become pregnant, they will automatically know if it will be a Martez or not. As for the men, we have to wait until we are twenty to figure out if the child is a Martez, even then it's not that accurate until the first power comes. If the child is like it's momma, then we don't know until it's 8 months old." He explained.

"Do you know how many there are?"

"There's 10, I only know the ones I have and I'm only twenty-three. The others are a complete mystery." He answered. "Any more questions?"

"No, that's all. But, can we go back to the house and may I marry your sister?"

"Yes, and definitely," Andrew flashed a smile before saying, "you're a good kid Stark. I'm sure you'll do everything in your power to keep her safe."

"Thank you, and that's the hope."

"No problem, and I think you'll do a good job. But speaking of, because of your make out sessions, you'll know if she's in danger or scared. You'll get a bad feeling in your stomach."

I was back at Saylor's house, following the loud music leading to Taylor's playroom. When I got to the doorway I was unnoticed, Mia and Taylor were standing a few inches away from the tv doing karaoke, while Saylor was on the couch with a blanket. I walked in, and started going in the direction of the couch unnoticed; until Saylor saw me and smiled, in return I smiled back. When I sat down on the couch I faced her and wrapped my arms around her and put her in my lap, giving her a kiss on the forehead.

"Hey," she snuggled into me.

"I don't want to leave you," I mumbled.

"You don't have to leave right away or right now. We can go into my room," she told me.

"A while will turn into hours, but I do, the mall is going to close soon and it doesn't open on Sundays." I held her tightly and then released her, dropping my arms.

"Maybe you're right," her voice was calm, but it made me look down at her, seeing that she was looking up at me. I gave her a kiss on the lips and when I pulled away I knew she yearned for more.

I laughed and put my forehead on her shoulder, looking over at the girls. "Mia, ready to go?"

"Yea," Mia turned and nodded.

"Ok, let's go," I gave Saylor a kiss on the cheek and looked her in the eye. "Be careful Peppermint."

"Alright, tell me the whole story. From the beginning," Landon demanded. We were in his room while Landon's little sister, Cleo, who was roughly Mia's age, and Mia were outside playing in the sprinklers.

"Well, when I first arrived to the school; Bella was the first person who helped me. Then I met you, but also, Bella always seemed pretty and beautiful to me, especially with her olive colored skin. Even if she has orange eyes, they're gorgeous and unique." I began, it was hard for me to call Saylor by her protective name, but it made perfect sense. I wanted to keep her safe, as much as it was weird.

"Alright, continue on," Landon nodded his head taking note of what I was saying.

"When you and your friends, at the time, were teasing me because I was defending her, I got fed up with that stuff. It wasn't until I beat some of them up and went to the office with a bloody nose that I asked her out. Ever since, we were, but we weren't official, we kept it to ourselves to prevent rumors. Though she was already getting them spread about her, I think she was afraid of them getting worse. Up until now, our relationship is public." I finished, soon adding, "just don't tell my dad."

"Okay, why not?" Landon smiled.

"I don't want my dad knowing all about the people I interact with, especially Bella. He doesn't act like he cares about us and he treats women with disrespect. I really want my mom to divorce him, I don't even know why she's still with him." I explained with a sigh.

"Alright man, I understand." He patted my back, which I didn't know if that caused my stomach to ache.

"Cool, thank you," I coughed out, hoping the ache would pass.

"No problem, you good though?" Landon wondered.

"Yea, just my stomach. Hopefully it'll pass."

The feeling did fade, and then an hour and a half later the pain came back, but more powerful. Then the gut feeling came a second later, a bad one. Andrew's words soon came to mind while I was playing Call Of Duty Black ops 2. Just as Landon and I were going to win, I froze.

"Bella." I said, stone cold in my voice.

Bella/Saylor:

"So, I can get whatever I want at the mall?" Taylor asked from her car seat in the back.

"Whatever you want, Pumpkin," I told her, concentrating on parking more than my niece.

"Yay!" She exclaimed.

"Alright, and we are good to get out." I leaned back in my seat, relieved at my parking job.

"Then get me out!" She whined.

"Pumpkin, no whining," I warned, unbuckling myself and getting out of the car.

Driving was not my favorite thing to do, actually, it was my least favorite thing to do. When I went around the car to get Taylor I saw some seventeen to eighteen year old boys on the other side of the parking lot. Since they were high school immature boys, they noticed me and couldn't help talking about how 'fine' my legs were and how 'hot' my body was. Regardless if it was winter or summer, whatever I wore was a lose-lose situation. I wasn't surprised that they were also talking about my ass as well. However, the conversation changed from 'fucking me' to me getting 'knocked up' when I pulled Taylor out of the car.

"Ugh, boys." I muttered with an eye roll. I propped Taylor up on my left while I closed her side of the door and locked the car. As we were heading in the direction of JC Penney's, the idiot guys started walking over to us.

"Hey baby," one of them said.

My first attempt was to ignore them, if I got too angry or scared I could end up giving Taylor a first degree burn.

"Come now hunny," another said.

"Leave me alone." I said sternly.

"Are you taken by anybody?" The third asked.

"I wonder what you'd be like in bed, with a body like that..." The first one smiled. You'd think that I didn't feel the fourth one behind me. His breathing heavily, though it could be my hearing that made it feel so loud.

"Get out of my way!" I yelled, fear creeping up on me. I couldn't show it, my hands starting to heat up. Soon Taylor would be getting warm, and I didn't need that happening.

"Ooo~ feisty." The one from behind me seemed amused. I couldn't act fast enough before he put his hands on my hips. I was still lucky to have the mix of Bella and Saylor, although it was not a good mix.

I closed my eyes and took a deep breath, exhaling before saying, "you won't hurt the child will you?"

"We don't want to do any harm, beautiful," the fourth guy whispered in my ear, his hands still lingering on my hips.

"Taylor, listen to me ok?" I started to whisper.

"Mhm," she nodded.

"I'm going to put you down, and you're going to run to the nearest lady that looks close enough to your mother's age. You're going to tell her that your auntie is getting harassed by guys," I finished whispering, leaning back a little, soon remembering that the guy was still behind me. "Can you do that?"

"Yea," she whimpered, she was scared too. I gave her a kiss on the forehead and put her down. To my relief she did as she was told and ran to the entrance.

"Where'd you send your daughter?" Idiots. Taylor barely looked like me, even if she had black hair like I used to have. Other than that, she looked more like her mother; blue eyes, light tan skin, and straight black hair with the orange highlights. It made Andrew and I worry that she was going to be like us. She hadn't gotten her phoenix tattoo yet, but I didn't get mine until I was five; her birthday was coming up though so we'd find out then. I was happy that our younger sister's weren't even like us.

"Are you going to answer us?!" The first guy barked, making me flinch. I couldn't have Saylor disappear on me now, especially since I needed her strength and her badass self to take over.

"None of your business." I said through gritted teeth.

For some reason this made them smile. I had to fight now, it was unfortunate that I haven't had to fight in a really long time because I knew I was weak. But, now I actually had to protect myself from my physical and mental self. I had nobody else to help me, I did have a four year old, but how fast could she get to someone?

I took a step back, the fourth guy still behind me with his hands on my hips. I stomped on his foot and elbowed him in the stomach.

"Arg!" He growled, stepping away, his hands were I elbowed him.

But that's where I was done. The third guy grabbed me by the waist from behind me, his hands tightly around my waist. The other two guys smiled and came up to me.

Saylor completely disappeared, I was helpless, scared. Just as the boys could do whatever they pleased; Taylor, a young woman, and a security guard came running towards us. The boys tried running off, but it was only seconds later that other cops and security guards were surrounding them. The security guards were soon taking care of them while the young lady was making sure I was ok.

"Did they hurt you?"

"No."

"Are you traumatized?"

"A little."

"Where are your parents?"

"Dead, but I'm living with my brother and his family."

"Do you have a boyfriend?"

"Yes."

"If he were to touch you, would you flinch?"

I didn't know how to respond to that one, "maybe. I plan on telling him as soon as I can."

"When's the next time you're gonna see him? Do you know?"

"I-I don't know. Tomorrow?"

"Are you okay?"

"I will be."

"Do you want me to stay with you girls and walk around with you?"

"Um," I was hesitant.

"Please auntie," Taylor's cold hand touched my leg, and I couldn't help but hear the shakiness of her voice.

"Yes please, thank you."

"Are you ready then? Or do you still need a moment?"

"I think I'm good," I smiled.

"Alright, where to first?" She asked.

"Build-A-Bear!" Taylor cheered. So we headed in that direction.

As we were walking around I learned that the young woman's name was Scarlet and she was 22. I also went through something similar to me, but there was nobody to help her so she ended up having twins. A girl, Aubrey and a boy, Carson.

We shopped for about an hour and a half before it happened. Before my whole life fell to pieces. Before I spent my days in a hospital, not even wanting to go to school. Before I saw my future crash and burn. Before Scarlet became Taylor's new babysitter. Before Sabrina and Andrew were never at the house because they were working 24/7 earning enough money to help Stark's mom. Before I thought I was going to graduate high school without my boyfriend there to congratulate and celebrate with me.

"I'm going to the bathroom real quick, okay?" Scarlet told us, looking from me to Taylor.

"Okay, I'm sure we'll be fine." I smiled, oh how wrong I was.

"Auntie Bella, can we get ice cream when she comes back?" Taylor asked.

"Sure," I answered. Then a guy came up to us, eyeing me suspiciously.

"Hey kids," he greeted. He was tall, had dark brown hair that oddly reminded me of Stark.

"Hi," I said skeptically.

"Where are your parents?" He wondered, looking around.

"At home," I responded, not trusting him at all.

"What about your house?" He questioned.

"Why would I tell you?" I was only getting a little scared.

"Because I'm a security guard here and I like getting to know my community." He smiled, but I didn't trust it and it was easy to tell that Taylor was scared as well.

"Then where's your uniform?" I asked, holding Taylor closer to me.

"I'm undercover. In fact you don't happen to know a girl named Saylor Martez do you? She has orange eyes and kinda looks like you, except for the hair." The guy explained, glancing at Taylor.

My heart rate increased, he is trying to look for me. He's no security guard, I didn't know it at first, but now I actually recognized him. He was the guy that killed my parents.

"Taylor, take my phone, and call daddy. He'll be Andrew in my phone but call him. Go into the bathroom with Scarlet and tell her to stay in the bathroom with her. Have daddy talk to Scarlet, explain everything that has happened ok?" I whispered to Taylor and gave her my phone.

"Mhm," she nodded and ran into the women's restroom.

I took a deep breath in and exhaled slowly looking back at the monster.

"I don't know this Saylor girl. Why are you looking for her?" I wondered. He looked at me suspiciously, studying me.

"What I've gathered about the Martez family is that they're really bad at lying. Saylor." He said my name through clenched teeth.

"My life isn't going to end, it'll be fine." I whispered to myself.

But, I was wrong. It was going to end one way or another. If I survived or not. Who knew that when you love someone so much your whole body is in pain and you feel like your life is going to end when they're the ones injured? He took a bullet to the stomach for me, he lost a lot of blood because of me. Everyone I loved always disappeared because of me. I **am** a danger to the world.

CHAPTER

4

Stark:

"Bro, explain this all to me! How do you know Bella or Saylor is in danger!" Landon asked. I was speeding all the way to the mall, trying to fill Landon in about Saylor.

"Because, her brother told me that since we've been having physical contact with each other, I'll know when she's scared or in danger. She was scared earlier before we started playing Call of Duty. She's probably in danger or scared now."

"Okay, can you slow down at all? A cop is gonna pull us over."

"No, if anything I'll be leading them to what actually matters."

When we got to the mall, without any cops, surprisingly, I saw Andrew speeding here too. Although he actually had a few cops behind them.

"Andrew!" I called running over to him.

"I was expecting to see you here," he nodded in my direction.

"Do you know what happened? Are the girls okay?" I asked.

"No time to talk, you need to be up there fast!" He put his hands on my shoulders and looked me dead in the eye.

Everything happened so fast, Andrew told me where Saylor was and I ran to her. I ran like my life depended on it. The whole time I was running my stomach got worse, it would say the least to even describe how it felt. It made each step seem like my life did depend on it, and made me wonder if a Martez soulmate ever died.

When I got to her she was curled up in a ball, looking weak. The guy, wait, the guy holding a gun at her he, that was my father. I didn't know how to even feel about that, but I had to put my own problems away. Everyone else in the mall looked scared, terrified even. What made me turn my attention back to Saylor and my father was the sound of the trigger getting pulled back. All he had to do was release the trigger and my whole world would fall dark.

"Dad!" I yelled, running over in front of Saylor.

"Stark?" I heard a faint whisper from her.

"Stark?! What on earth are you doing here?! Get away from her! She's dangerous!" Although my dad looked all burned he was still standing and was able to use his commanding voice that was used with every argument in my house.

"I'm not going anywhere, she is my girlfriend! And I love her!" I glared at him.

"You'd rather risk your life for her?! Are you out of your mind?!"

"Yes, I'd do anything to protect her and would you really shoot your own son? And to be clear, I am not out of my mind. She may have powers, but it's not like she uses them all the time. The powers don't matter to me, it's her being her true self, it's the inside that matters to me."

"Stark, don't do this. Be smart, you protected me long enough. There's other girls that are better for you. Andrew also wants me to tell you that he's almost near." Her voice was so weak, the agony was too much to carry. I wished it could be done sooner. I just had to keep distracting him a little bit more and he'd be caught.

"Dad, I'd rather risk my life for her because she actually cares about me. I love her so much that I want to marry her. Shoot me instead of her. Take my life instead of hers."

"Stark, she's manipulative, can't you see? She's got you right where she wants you to be. After you risk your life for her, she's going to leave you. And she won't even care." His betrayed eyes lowered to the floor by my feet and the gun lowered, the bullet was released.

I looked to see where it was headed. She moved. It was going straight to her.

"No!" I dropped to the floor in front of her, just as the bullet hit my stomach.

Beep, beep, beep. I opened my eyes, a room full of white, flower, and 'get well' balloons, plus a machine that wouldn't stop beating, causing one hell of a headache. This was just a plain ol' boring hospital room. All white, with the only colored areas being the flowers, balloons, and my peppermint who was curled up in a ball beside me, using my arm as a pillow.

She was wearing black sweatpants and a sweatshirt, her feet being the only thing not covered other than the blanket she used to cover her feet. They were against mine, and the heat radiated off to where I was all nice and warm as well. Her sleep was just as peaceful before I left to see Landon, her eyes closed, slowly breathing, and her mouth slightly open. It was nice seeing her like this again.

"You're awake," I didn't even notice Landon in the corner of the room, sitting in a chair.

"Yea, I guess so," it was weird talking, I kinda didn't recognize my own voice.

"How do you feel?" He asked, walking over to me.

"Little pain, not much though," I answered.

"Must be the medicine, let me know if it hurts more, I can call a nurse." His voice was also different, much calmer.

"How are you?" I wondered.

"I'm doing good. Saylor has been through a lot, but she's pretty cool." He sighed, looking at my baby.

"What happened? What's been going on? How long have I been here for?" I was worried now.

"After you got shot, the police and Andrew were able to catch your dad. Saylor, however, though she was weak, cried on you, she cried until she fell asleep in the car on the way to the hospital. Taylor and Scarlet, which I'll have Saylor tell you about, they went home with Sabrina. Your dad is in prison for life, and Saylor is no longer in danger." He paused to catch his breath.

"At least Saylor isn't in danger anymore," I mumbled.

"Yeah, you've been out for a few months, it's almost graduation and Saylor's birthday is coming up. Anyways over those months Saylor and I have gotten to know each other really well. I judged her too quickly, she's a really cool girl. But, we've been coming here everyday, sometimes she'll skip school and sometimes she'll stay the night too." He explained.

"Dang, I missed a lot, I can't imagine what Peppermint has been through," I sighed, hating what happened. If I went to school that Friday like she told me to, none of this would have happened.

"Sometimes I'd find her at my door in tears. Sabrina and Andrew are now working 24/7 helping your mom, helping you. They still do their college but they're never really home," Landon frowned.

"Oh Saylor," I frowned, looking down at her. She was still sleeping peacefully.

"I'm learning to know her, she stands up for everyone just in the distance. Plus, she gets a pretty unique personality. She's perfect for you," Landon smiled.

"She's changing you too," I smiled.

"Yea, I guess so," he laughed.

Bella/Saylor:

"I want everything to go back to how it was," I whispered.

"That would be nice," he agreed as he kept moving his hand on my bare shoulder. I was only wearing Saylor's favorite bra and jeans. My shirt was on Stark's chair in his room, one word did repeat in my mind though.

"Would?" I now had both of my hands on his chest and my chin resting on them.

"Think on the positive, without that happening you and Landon would still probably not be friends." He explained.

"Okay, right now, I'm glad that the hospital let you go home. Even if you have a house nurse," I sighed, not liking his response.

"Same, it's nice being home and in comfortable clothes and setting." He smiled, moving a strand of my hair behind my hair.

"Ask me questions, I know you have them," I confronted.

"Okay, how did you meet Scarlet? How did you become so weak? And lastly, how were you while I was out?" He questioned.

"One question at a time," I laughed, though letting it die remembering everything that happened that day. "When I got to the mall, and got out of the car, there were these guys, roughly our age."

He started to tense.

"Chill, when I got Taylor out of the car they came up to us. They nearly harassed me. I had Taylor go and find somebody to help; I tried fighting them, but they were too fast. Luckily, Taylor came back with Scarlet and a security guard. That is how I met Scarlet."

"I don't trust her." He said flatly, soon asking, "What happened to the guys."

"One, you haven't even met her or talked to her. Two, she got harassed but it went too far that she ended up having twins. Three, the guys are in jail for a year and a half." I explained.

"One, I still don't trust her. Two, I'm glad that those guys are in jail. Three, think you can answer my next question?" He sighed, taking one of my hands and kissed my knuckles.

"I became so weak because I used up all my powers on your dad. I have practiced my powers throughout my life and each time I use them I grow tired and weak. When I used them on your dad, I gave it all I could and almost passed out."

"Hm, hopefully you don't have to use that much of your power anymore." Stark looked up at his ceiling, tightly closing his eyes like he was in pain. He still had my hand in his, and if he knew it or not, he was squeezing my hand tightly.

"What's wrong?!" I shot up, sitting up. "What hurts?"

"Get me the pain reliever medicine," he said through clenched teeth.

"Okay," I got up, let my hand free, and went to get his medicine.

"Thank you," he thanked after taking another sip of water.

"Of course," I gave a small smile. He was now sitting up, the nurse was replacing his bandages.

"There you go, all set. Just stay sitting up," the nurse smiled at Stark then to me and left the room.

"Well, we can still be comfortable," I shrugged and moved pillows to the corner of the wall.

"True," Stark smiled and leaned back against them while I snuggled up next to him. "Can I get my last two questions answered?"

"Yea," I smiled. "Landon helped me a lot while you were in the hospital. I told him about what happened and how I met Scarlet. He was the only person who was there for me while everyone else was busy. He's a good friend to have." I answered.

"He is, I could tell that you've already changed him. You've actually changed me as well." Stark put his head against mine.

"Really?"

"Yea, last question; how were you while I was out?"

"I was a mess. I cried almost all the time. School was difficult, but I still went and lasted the whole day. I'd go and visit you or Landon But it was tough, somedays I didn't want to get out of bed. It was easy to drown in tears when I was alone. But I hated it."

"I'm never gonna leave you, remember that. I'll love you even when I become six feet under." He gave me a kiss on the cheek.

"I love you too," I whispered, snuggling deeper next to him and moving myself to face his side. I closed my eyes and relaxed.

CHAPTER

5

Stark:

I want to graduate High School with my Peppermint. The only way to do that was by hiring a personal teacher. Even if I am defined as the "popular guy" at school, I still paid attention in class and got A's and B's.

So, since graduation was a month and a week away, I've been getting all the help I can get. I have a teacher and then I have a Saylor too. I'm a fast learner so we've been going pretty fast. I'm having to take tests and quizzes along with the other stuff as well.

Saylor's stressing a little, she said I was the only person that made her be able to relax and feel stress free with. Which could be the reason why she stays at my house more than her own. I also found out that Sabrina is working extra hours and finding a job to work full time on; she just graduated from her 4-year college. With the extra money she's helping my mom with the hospital bills and stuff.

While Andrew is working a part time job to help me buy Saylor a ring. My plan is to purpose a month after her birthday. I know that I'm going to end up using all of my money and we might not have a wedding ceremony right away. But, it's worth the wait, especially with all the things going on right now. I'm surprised that Saylor hadn't mentioned it yet. The fact that I did mention it. But, she was weak, and so much has happened, that I'm hoping she forgot about it.

I haven't been in that much pain. It's been three weeks since I was last at the hospital, even then the doctor said I was fine and I'd be all healed by the end of the month. Until then I have to rest and make sure the bandages don't get too bloody.

Mia has been trying to cope with everything that's been going on. Sometimes she comes in my room when she thinks I'm asleep and she'll cry, talk, or curl up next to me and will fall asleep. She has also been hanging out with Landon's sister too.

Taylor has been good, I think. Saylor will still talk about her every so often. What I don't like is Scarlet babysitting Taylor. I get a bad feeling from her, but I also haven't seen Taylor. It was only once, and that was when I was in the hospital.

My mom has been alright. Every so often she'll come and check on me. I know she's worried about me, but having Saylor here, she's been a little bit more happier. My mom still goes to work, and I know she's happy with her friends and doing what she loves to do.

"Stark!! Focus!!" Saylor whined, throwing her head back.

"I'm sorry babe!" I apologized.

"It's fine, is the pain a distraction for you?" She sighed, leaning back up next to me.

"No, if anything it'd be you," I teased with a wink.

"Sure," She rolled her eyes at me.

"When's the essay due?" I was all caught up in English, my easy subject along with my electives.

"In two days, you're good at peer editing and helping me, but you're so distracted today." She complained.

"Hey, you'll turn it in on time," I comforted.

"Says the one who's my peer editor and you've already turned yours in already," she grumbled.

"Take a nap, I'll be done by the time you wake up," I advised.

"Fine," she mumbled, laying down behind me on my pillow.

I smiled and started to take a look at her essay. When I was done I looked back at Saylor to see her still sleeping. I put my computer over on my desk and laid next to her, wrapping my arms around her, pulling her against me, and closed my eyes.

"Do you want to see your father?" My mom asked. Saylor, Mia, my mom, and I were all in the dining room eating dinner.

"Why? He nearly killed Bella and he's a horrible father." I shook my head not understanding why she'd ask such a silly question.

"He wants to see you. He said he had something important to tell you." My mom sighed.

"What could that possibly be?" I rolled my eyes.

"He said it had something to do with Bella." As soon as she finished her sentence I tensed up. My Saylor? What could it possibly be? She couldn't be in danger anymore right? Unless…

"Okay, I'll see him. But he tells me the important thing first and then that's it." I gave in, my voice a little commanding.

"That's fine," my mom nodded.

"Stark, I want to talk to you when we're done eating," Saylor looked over at me.

I nodded in response. When we finished eating, Saylor and I got in Saylor's car and we took a ride to a hill we found while I was in 'bed rest'. It was the only way to get away from the nurse, we couldn't go to Saylor's because we already tried and the nurse found us. So, by going to the hill, nobody knew where we were, Andrew did, and he didn't care. After all, 'he remembers his teenage years', he mentioned that he ended up injuring himself, that he ended up being on bed rest while he was with Sabrina. The hill was a great place to watch the sunset and the sunrise.

"What did you want to talk about?" I wondered once we got to the hill.

"I want to change my name back to Saylor Martez and I want your opinion on it," she answered.

"No." Was my immediate response.

"Why? It's not like I'm in danger any more. Plus, I thought you liked calling me Saylor," she looked at me confused.

I looked out at the view of the houses and buildings as I explained, "we don't know if you are still in danger or not. Sure my dad is gone, but there could still be people out there looking for you. Plus I really don't trust Scarlet. What if she works with my dad? I get a bad feeling with her."

"But she helped me and my brother trusts her! Taylor feels safe around her!" She complained.

"No, your brother doesn't trust her. He only agreed to have Scarle babysit Taylor because he and Sabrina are both working and he knew you wouldn't be able to handle taking care of her since you were worrying about me and school." I told her, now looking at her.

"Stark," she started, her voice getting whiny like she was going to cry. But, she is on her menstrual cycle so I shouldn't have been surprised.

I sighed, "Change your name to Saylor Larren. It'd be better and that is what I'll agree to. I wanna keep you safe, I'm trying to keep you safe. But, that can't happen unless you help me keep you safe."

"I will change my name to Saylor Larren."

Bella/Saylor:

Staring at myself in my mirror, wearing a black cap and gown. For the first time in a long time I pulled my hair back into a high ponytail. Under the gown was a white dress that had purple flowers on it, it reached down to my knees. There were no straps and my shoes were white flats.

I was finally able to change my name to Saylor Larren; the whole school now knew my new full name. I was glad that Stark and I were able to agree on letting me change my name.

I'm also glad that Stark is all healed and is able to graduate High School with me. Stark found out that he will be able to visit his dad in three months.

"Saylor! Come on! We can't be late!" Andrew yelled from the stairs.

"Coming!" I yelled back, taking one look at myself and leaving my room.

The ceremony felt like it went by too fast. I enjoyed every little thing that happened. Though, in the audience I saw three girls who seemed familiar along with two younger girls as well. All five of them were sitting with Andrew and the rest of the family, including Mr. Leon and Stark and Landon's as well. After the ceremony we stayed at the school for a while to take pictures and hang out with family. There was going to be a party at the park at noon.

I was getting myself a cupcake from the table which had treats on it that people brought when Stark came up next to me and nudged my shoulder.

"So, college student, do you know what you want to be when you are looking for a job?" He asked.

"Someone who works in a pet shelter, taking care of all the animals," I answered, grabbing a cupcake with one hand and taking Stark's hand with the other. Starting to walk over to Andrew and the rest of the families.

"You can't get used to the animals," he warned.

"I know," I nodded. "What do you want to be?"

"Detective or police officer," he said without any hesitation.

"Alright, how long have you been thinking about that?" I wondered.

"Since I really found out how much danger you can be in," he smiled.

"Impossible," I rolled my eyes while a laugh escaped. I knew he wanted to protect me, but I didn't realize how much he wanted to. I looked up at him, he was just smiling, his eyes trying to tell me something. The look made my heart do something it's never really done before, it's so hard to explain.

We know made it to my brother and everyone else, but our eyes still kept eye contact. Stark was still giving me a smile and his eyes were still trying to tell me something. I was looking at him with probably a confused look, still trying to figure out what his eyes were telling me.

But, while I was trying to find the answer, it ended up getting ended.

"Auntie Saylor!" Taylor flung her arms around me.

Ever since she ended up getting her phoenix tattoo Andrew and I had to explain that we had to hide who we were. I explained why Stark ended up in the hospital and why his dad was after me. I told her my real name and what happened to her grandparents on our side, it was really sad to tell her, it was the one day I stayed home instead of going to the hospital to see Stark.

"Hi pumpkin," I looked down at her smiling and picked her up hugging her close to me.

"Hey Taylor," Stark waved.

"Starky!!" Taylor reached out to Stark who grabbed her and put her on the side of him. Leaving me childless. "I'm glad you're finally healed up."

"Thanks kiddo," he smiled then looked over at me. "How are you doing Peppermint?"

"I'm good, really, I am." I smiled, now admiring the way Stark and Taylor interacted with each other. Wondering how he'd be when we had- wait, what am I thinking??

"Hey, Saylor, I flew out some girls here and I'm hoping you remember them," Andrew nudged my shoulder, making my attention go towards the familiar girls.

"You girls do look familiar," I smiled. They were looking back at me.

The one in the middle had blue eyes and curly dark brown hair that had dark blue highlights. She was wearing an all black crop top, cut out sleeves on the shoulder, and her shoulder went down to her elbow. She had a black skirt with black heels.

The girl to the right of her head hazel eyes with blonde straight hair, her highlights were a light brown. The blonde and brown highlights looked really good with her. This girl was wearing a sleeveless dress, an orange creamy color that reached her shins. Her shoes were also white, but sandals.

Realization hit with a blink of an eye.

I didn't even have to look at the girl to the left of Rachel to know that she'd have her black wavy hair that has purple highlights pulled back into a ponytail. I knew that she had dark brown eyes filled with fierceness like she always did. Since I knew her so well she'd be wearing black long boots that reached her knee caps and dark purple short shorts that matched with a dark blue button tank top which was all the way unbuttoned and tied at the stomach showing off her favorite black sports bra.

I smiled at all three of them, tears of joy escaping my eyes, a laugh also escaping my mouth.

"She knows," Carly looked over at the other two smiling.

"How is this possible? I thought I'd never see you girls again!" I was shocked.

"Can you give us a hug first? We miss you," Lola, the one to the right of Rachel asked in her child-like voice. The voice that made Carly, Rachel, and I have to stick up to the punk kids. From the day I met her I loved her personality, I can only hope that her free spirit personality didn't change. Even if she did change, I'd still love her.

"We're still waiting on an answer Chica, we've missed you." Rachel opened her arms.

"Yes!" I nodded, laughing and running over to them. "I missed you guys too!"

"Sooo, you and Stark found each other again?" Carly nudged me after we hugged. I smiled and looked at Stark who was messing around with Taylor, he caught me looking at him and he smiled. His smile took my breath away, and it was getting difficult to look at him.

I cleared my throat and looked back at the girls, "yea, it was hard at first."

"You couldn't tell him who you were right away?" Carly asked.

"No, I had to do everything to protect myself," I sighed. "You guys, know what happened right?"

"They do, after you came here I kept in touch with them and kept them updated." Andrew came to my side.

"Thank you, this all makes sense now," again tears were in my eyes as I pulled my girls into another group hug.

"We also have a surprise for you," Rachel leaned back with a smile.

"Girls, come here," Lola waved two other girls over. The one's I also saw.

"Oh my gosh," I nearly cried again.

"Hold up, are they who I think they are?" Stark came to my side, putting his hand on my shoulder. Taylor was back on her own two feet standing next to him.

"Yea, I think so." I nodded, kneeling to the ground, Stark coming down with me.

"Sissy?" Alexis mumbled, questionly.

"Come here girls," I cried out, opening my arms out to them.

"Saylor!" Ella sobbed running into my arms. The same with her twin.

"Oh, babies, I missed you guys so much!" I cried happy tears, holding them and never wanting to let go.

"You girls got so big!" Stark said in awe.

"Well, they are eight now." Carly mentioned.

"Stark!!" The girls leaned out of my arms and went over to Stark.

"Why don't we hit the park and celebrate?" I suggested, not wanting this day to end.

"Sounds good!" Andrew nodded. Andrew took Sabrina, Taylor, Ella, and Alexis in his car, Rachel had her license and was able to get a rental car so the three girls drove in there, while Stark and I rode together in his car. Once we got to the park my girls plus Stark and I found a bench to sit at, and started to catch up.

"So, what's new with you girls?!" I exclaimed, leaning forward.

"Well, for starters, Lola and I are together," Rachel smiled, blush filling her cheeks.

"Finally! It took a while!" I cheered. "Did you guys do the little pack we made when you guys turned 18?"

"Maybe!" Rachel leaned back a little, lips pressed together. It was obvious to tell from both her face and Lola's that she did.

"Yea, she did." Carly rolled her eyes with a laugh.

"Did Lola?" I wondered.

"Of course I did, it wouldn't be a pack without it would it? At least we didn't do a blood pack." Lola nodded, and she too did an eye roll.

"Oh my gosh! How was it? Did you like it?" I asked eagerly.

"Honestly, it depends on the person," she told me.

"That makes sense?" I said, though confused.

"Lola dated someone before Rachel. That guy was her 18th birthday. But, he was awful! You would've hated him too, Saylor. If looks could kill," Carly explained with an eye roll. Now it made sense. Lola was the oldest of us all, then it was Rachel, then Carly, leading me to be the youngest.

"Well, Rachel did you like it though?" I looked over at Rachel.

"Yea, but I'll admit I was nervous," she answered.

"She was perfect though," Lola winked, making Rachel blush even more than she was.

"Alright twin, what about you??" I looked towards Carly and raised my eyebrow.

"Well, I still wanted to complete our pack and at the time I was single and smart. So, I went up to my super sweet guy friend, explained to him how stupid and crazy we were freshman year. He ended up agreeing to letting me do our pack and now he's my boyfriend!" Carly explained, soon looking over to Stark. "Plus, I bet that Stark remembers him."

"Aye, you got one of my old buddies? That's cool," he smiled.

"Damn twin, never thought you had time for a guy. Though since you did get one, I'm not surprised it's a softy though." I smiled with a wink.

"Alright, what about you? Are you still committing to our pack on your 18th birthday?" Rachel leaned in looking at me and taking a quick glance at Stark.

"Maybe, so much has happened, I haven't had time to even think about it. Plus, I don't have you girls here so I completely forgot about it in the first place." I shrugged, leaning my head on Stark's shoulder.

"Well, even with everything that has happened, I think you should figure out what you're gonna do. We all did our part of the pack, it's our leader's time to do the same." Carly crossed her arms and narrowed her eyes at me.

"How am I still the leader?? I haven't been with you girls for a year and a half!" I exclaimed.

"Cause, even with your new soft side, you're still the fiercest girl in our group. Nobody would be able to pull off what you can do. Powers aside, you always know what to say and what to do. You are a natural born leader," Lola explained, Rachel nodding along with agreement.

"Alright then, Carly, where's your softy?" I sat up straight and folded my hands.

"He didn't want to come, he still remembers you as the girl who would yell at guys for playing with a girl's heart. And the girl who got detention almost every week because you wouldn't follow the school's dress code." Carly answered.

"That's how I first met her," Stark mumbled.

"Yea," I rolled my eyes at him. But then asked, "Why didn't you pick it up again when you moved here?"

"Cause I already had my eyes set for you," he shrugged.

"Oh my goodness," I again rolled my eyes.

"Awww, I always loved you too," Lola beamed.

"I can see how Bella changed you though," Stark rubbed my shoulder. He already knew how much I didn't like the fact that Bella even changed me, or that I have two personalities.

"Yeah, she did. But, I still don't like it when a boy plays with a girl's heart." I agreed. "Did you tell your softy that I'm different?"

"We tried convincing him, even showing him some clips of the videos Andrew sent us wouldn't work!" Carly pouted.

"Girl, I don't think I've ever seen you pout," I squinted my eyes at her.

"This is what happens when her boyfriend isn't around when she really wants him," Rachel informed/

"You gotta be kidding me," I raised my eyebrows in disbelief, a little disappointed in Carly.

"Wish we were," Lola muttered.

"Carly!" I scowled looking over at her then passed her where I saw a boy walking over to us. He looked familiar but also unfamiliar, he had blonde hair and blue eyes, wearing a polo and jeans.

"Oh my goodness, your boyfriend is Devon!" Stark got all excited.

"I knew it!" I muttered.

"What? How on earth do you guys know?" Carly gasped.

"Close your eyes Chica," I smiled. Though she was confused, she listened and closed her eyes.

"Hey," Devon wrapped his arms around Carly's shoulder and gave her a kiss on the neck.

"Devon!" She opened her eyes and turned her head, facing Devon.

"Hi Carly," he laughed sitting next to her.

"So you're the softy, I knew you guys would be cute." I smiled at them. With Devon being next to Carly, my twin seemed to be a lot happier.

"I shouldn't be surprised that you gave me a nickname. Nice to see you too Saylor," Devon smiled, putting his arm around Carly's shoulder as she leaned into him.

Somehow, that made me jealous. Could they be cuter than Stark and I? Or was it because Stark didn't have his arm around me? When was the last time he had his arm around me? When was the last time we kissed or made out?

"Same to you," I gave a weak smile; hoping none of my friends or Stark didn't notice the weakness.

"It's nice seeing you old buddy, I'd love to stay here and chat some more; but I was wondering if I had some time with Saylor? I'd like to have her for the rest of the night, if that's okay of course," Stark spoke, making me realize he noticed.

. "Of course! She is yours after all, plus we did want to see Taylor, it's been too long." Carly nodded, smiling the whole time.

"Yea, the last time we saw her, she was only a baby," Lola agreed.

"I'll see you girls later," I got out of my seat, rolling my eyes.

"Bye Chica," Rachel smiled.

"Have fun!" Carly yelled as we were walking away.

"Oh my gosh," I laughed with an eye roll.

"I'm glad you got to see them, you seemed a lot more like yourself than you have been," Stark bumped my shoulder.

"It was really nice seeing them, though I like to pretend I don't know them sometimes." I bumped him back.

"Really?" This time he grabbed me and locked me in his arms, lifting me off the ground while we walked to his new truck.

"Hey!" I scowled.

"I'll be putting you down in a minute," he told me while I tried to squirm.

"You're mean," I grumbled.

"Uhuh," he agreed, giving me a kiss on the shoulder.

"I hate you," I muttered.

"Okay," he said this like he didn't believe me and gave me a kiss on the side of my neck.

"Ugh, you're impossible." I leaned back, closing my eyes.

"I know that, and the same to you. Now we're at the car so I'll put you down. Need any help?" He put me down and kissed the side of my head.

"I should be fine," I smiled, opening my door and stepping on the little ramp for a boost up. I soon got in my seat and closed my door, Stark got on the driver's side.

"Alright, next stop is our spot." Stark looked over at me as he finished buckling.

"Sounds good!" I smiled.

"Answer this question Peppermint," Stark whispered, his warm breath on my neck.

"Look at me and I'll answer it once you ask," I whispered back.

Stark sat up a little bit, putting his arms into a plank position on each side of my head. He looked down at me, desperate to kiss me some more.

"What is this 18th birthday pack you girls were talking about?" He asked.

"Surprised you don't know," I smiled.

"Tell me, I might have an idea, but I want to be sure."

"What's the idea?" I wondered, not knowing what I was getting myself into.

"This," he leaned back to my neck and gave me a kiss. Though this kiss was different than anything I've ever felt, hard but nice. I felt his hands slide down to my waist, starting to pull it up. He was too good at this, that my body lit up with sensation.

"Yes Stark! Yes, you're right!" I breathed out.

He kept his hands under my dress but leaned back and gave me a kiss, "so 18? In a few weeks?"

"Yes," I confirmed.

"Are you sure? I still plan to wait when you want to," he asked, being amazing.

"I think we deserve some fun after everything we've been through." I told him with a smile.

"Then I can't wait." He smiled back. Kiss, kiss, and then we were on our side, his arms around me, blankets on top of us, making me feel warm and safe.

"I needed this," I mumbled.

"I know."

CHAPTER

6

Stark:

Tomorrow is her birthday. I'm making sure that she completes her pack, after all if the other three have, she must. At least that's what her 'twin', Carly said. Honestly, I'm not surprised that this was their pack, giving up their virginity. With Saylor Martez being trouble and how they looked (not saying they looked like hoes) in that picture, I couldn't be surprised. We've made out several times and almost did end up losing our virginity, but this time around, I want to make sure that this is what Saylor wants and she's not doing it because she feels 'forced' or 'pressured' by her friends. Not to say that I'm nervous, but was Saylor? The Bella side of her? I always wanted this to be a natural thing to lose, but it is what it is. If this is what she wants, then I'll take it. It's not like I didn't plan on marrying her, she's my whole life.

"Are you ready for tomorrow?" I asked, rubbing my thumb against her cheek. We were on our hill on the tailgate of the truck. We had blankets and pillows surrounding us making it nice and comfortable to be.

"I think so," she turned on her back, looking up at the stars.

"You think so?" I slightly teased, raising my eyebrow.

"I never imagined what my 18th birthday would be like, other than having you there plus the girls. But, I never imagined my high school years. Or the fact that my parents wouldn't be there," she explained.

"Hey, hey, nobody expects these things. If it wasn't for finding you again, I would probably have reverted back to my old ways, along with graduating with C's." I wrapped my arms around her, pulling her close to me.

"Maybe you're right."

"I know I'm right, when I first met you I started working hard. Proving myself to be good enough for you. Pushing myself to be the best guy I can," I persuaded her.

"Alright, alright," she laughed. Which was nice to hear.

"Good, now, what's the plan for tomorrow?" I asked with a smile.

"Carly said that the girls were going to wake me up with blow horns at seven in the morning. From there we're going to hang out and have fun until 7:30 where I'll be with you." She answered.

"Alright, well, hopefully you have fun with the girls," I told her.

"Probably will," she shrugged.

"Are you ready for what I have planned?" I wondered, sitting up a little and looking down at her.

"Yes sir!" She smiled, putting her hands around my neck and pulling me in for a kiss. One way or another she got me to be on my back and had her on top of me.

"Hey, this ain't fair," I complained when she pulled away.

"It's almost my birthday, Starky Stark. I get to do whatever I want!" She sat up and put her hands on her hips.

"You're lucky you're gorgeous baby," I smiled up at her putting my hands on top of her hips which caused her to move hers and pulled her to me.

"Well, I am indeed gorgeous, so thank you!" She put her hands on my chest and kissed my neck, her teeth right against my skin when she pulled away.

"Babe, you have no idea how that feels," I closed my eyes, trying to concentrate on my breathing.

"There will be more of that tomorrow night," she remarked.

"I should just bring you home now so you can just get ready for bed and go to sleep. Tomorrow will come faster that way," I suggested.

"I might as well bring you to bed with me," she teased.

"Or we could just stay here and spend the night here. Your friends might miss the chance to wake you up with blow horns," I offered.

"You'll be bringing me home at some point," she rolled her eyes, sitting up, and getting off of me.

"Who said you could do that?" I asked, sitting up.

"Do what?" She looked back at me confused.

"Get off of me," I told her, leaning back on my elbows.

"I have to regain my self-control at some point," she smiled.

"What about tomorrow night?" I wondered.

"Ten percent self-control," she answered.

"Alright," I laughed. "Let me get you home, I still need to do a few things for tomorrow."

"Okay," she frowned, grabbing her shirt and putting it back on.

Bella/Saylor:

"It's time to get out of bed!" Lola grabbed my arm and tried to yank me out of bed.

"But I want to sleep! I went to bed at 12!" I complained.

"Well, you were making out with Stark for half an hour outside the house," Carly stated and sat on me.

"Now I really can't get up." I buried my head in my pillows," where's Rachel?"

"Right here Chica, Carly grab her legs." Rachel ordered as I felt Cary get off of me and grabbed my legs. Rachel and Lola grabbed my wrists, they lifted me out of bed and put me on the floor.

"Alright, I'll get up," I sighed and stood up.

"Happy 18th birthday!" The girls squealed and gave me a hug.

"Thank you," I smiled.

"Now, the first thing on the list is for you to shower and brush your teeth; while we pick your outfit out for the day then we'll do your hair," Carly grabbed my arm and shoved me out of my room.

"When you're done in the shower put your undies and bathrobe on, then brush your teeth. After you're done with that, come back in here," Lola explained, giving me my bathrobe and a new pair of undies.

"Alright," I sighed and went into my bathroom, closing the door. I heard the girls giggle as I started the shower.

"And allll done!" Lola smiled looking up at the mirror.

"You girls are crazy," I looked at myself in the mirror. A black silk skirt, dark red crop top, and my hair was pulled back into a ponytail.

"We know," they beamed. I couldn't help but to smile with them.

"Now step 3, breakfast that Andrew made!" Carly grabbed my hand and pulled me all the way down stairs to the dining room.

"Wow," my eyes went wide as my dining table was all decorated and Andrew just placed a batch of warm buttery pancakes on the table.

"Happy 18th birthday Saylor Martez-Larren," Andrew smiled.

"Thanks," I thanked, sliding into my seat.

"Yes, thank you for breakfast," Rachel nodded as the rest of the girls sat in their chairs.

"Taylor, Sabrina, Alexis, Ella, and I will stay out of your way," Andrew told us and then left the room.

"So, what's next on the list?" I wondered.

"A movie, walk, and some place to get lunch, some games, and then we get you ready for Stark." Carly answered, listing everything on her fingers.

"Okay." I took a deep breath in then out, today was going to be a long day.

After we ate we watched two Twilight movies and then decided to take a walk.

"What is your favorite place to eat at?" Lola asked.

"That is close by," Rachel added.

"California Burgers. They have a variety of food, and they're amazing!" I replied with a smile on my face

"Well, lead the way, we'll have that for lunch!" Carly pushed me to the front and walked next to me with her elbow on my shoulder. "Are you ready for tonight?"

"Yes," I nodded.

"You'll be taking his breath away for sure," Carly smiled.

"Oh that's nice, what are you going to do?" I rolled my eyes.

"Dress you up in a dark red dress, you are 18 so you can show off your phoenix. Your hair is going to be curled and you'll be wearing black high heel boots." Carly explained.

"You guys are crazy," I sighed.

"Oh, but you love us," Carly teased.

"That I do," I sighed again.

After we ate, we played many games including Uno and Janga. As we were playing we also watched more Twilight until it was 7. The girls made me shower again and then got me all ready.

"Wow," Rachel took a step back, her hand on her mouth.

"Oh my," Lola bit the bottom of her lip, smiling.

"Let me know when to say I told you so," Carly was awed to, but not as much.

"You may be right," I laughed out. We all looked in the mirror, admiring how magnificent I looked.

"I missed you looking like this," Lola smiled, finally being able to speak a full sentence.

"Me too," I agreed.

"Can we toss all of Bella's clothes out and go shopping for new ones?" Carly wondered.

"Hey, Bella and Saylor both love her clothes," I felt offended.

"Okay, okay. Plus you do have some pretty cute and cool clothing," Carly beamed.

The door then rang and I heard Andrew answer it.

"Stark's here," I bit the bottom of my lip, now feeling nervous.

"Ready?" Rachel asked, "bag all packed?"

"Yes." I nodded with a smile.

"Wow." Was the first thing Stark said when he saw me come down the stairs.

"I know," I agreed, smiling and walking up to him.

"You look amazing," he smiled back.

"Thank you, you're not that bad either," I gave him a once over. He was wearing black jeans, white button up, and his hair was a mess. "Am I overdressed?"

"A little, but you look great so don't worry about it." He shrugged, "ready to go?"

"Yea," I nodded.

"Bye," Carly came behind me, giving me a backwards hug.

"Bye girls," I turned to wave as Stark and I headed out the door.

"How has your birthday been so far?" Stark asked once he started the car.

"It's been good, watched movies, played games, we went to California Burgers for lunch," I explained.

"Nice, so, do you think a picnic on the tailgate at our hill is ok?" Stark wondered.

"It sounds good," I smiled.

"Cool."

"Do you dance?" Stark questioned, we were sitting on the tailgate relaxing and talking after our little romantic dinner.

"After three years of knowing me, you don't know the answer to that question?"

"Nope," Stark shrugged.

"No, and I won't ever," I shook my head.

"I'm going to turn that into a lie," Stark grinned and got off the tailgate.

"What?" I gasped.

"Come on," Stark waved his hand. "I'm going to teach you."

"Fine," I sighed, knowing I wasn't going to get out of it.

"Come," we walked over to the side of the truck. Stark put music on his phone and then grabbed my waist and pulled me close to him. "Put your arms around my neck and then sway to the music."

"Like this?" I guessed as I did what he told me.

"Yep! Exactly like this," he smiled excitedly.

"Is this your favorite way to dance?" I asked.

"Mmm, why do you ask?"

"Because I know there are more ways to dance than this one."

"Well, then let's say yes. It is my favorite way to dance." He pulled me closer to him until our bodies were touching.

I looked up at him as he looked down at me. I went on my tippy toes and gave him a kiss, touching his bottom lip with my tongue as I pulled away. Next thing I knew, I was against the truck getting hard, passionate kisses.

From what I thought was an hour or two passed, we were curled up on the tailgate. I was in my undies, bra, and Stark's crisp white button-up shirt while Stark was in his sweatpants that he packed.

"So now we just stay here and spend the night here?" I asked.

"Yea, is that ok?" Stark wondered.

"That's perfect, this is the first time we're sleeping up here." I said.

"Hopefully it's comfortable," Stark nuzzled his face into the back of my neck.

"Are you comfortable?"

"Yea, you?"

"Yea."

"Happy Birthday Peppermint."

"Thanks."

"I love you Saylor."

"I love you Stark."

CHAPTER

7

Stark:

It's been a month since Saylor's birthday. Today would be the last day I pulled my last move, maybe. She was the one girl who changed me for the better.

The one girl who was kept close to my heart, closer than my mom and sister. She was now part of my life and she was always going to stay that way. I found the perfect ring for her and I just have to hope that she'll say yes.

"She's gonna say yes idiot, but good speech." Carly punched my shoulder. I didn't realize that I had spoken those words out loud until now.

"Why are you now starting to call me that? Plus, aren't you supposed to be back at your home getting ready for college?" I looked over at Carly who was making herself lunch.

We were all at Saylor's house; Taylor, Alexis, Ella, and Mia, were upstairs hanging out in Taylor's playroom. Rachel and Lola were getting Saylor ready for our date. Devon was sitting next to me across from Carly. We have all gotten used to each other's relationship status. Before Saylor and I left, we were the only people in a relationship and Devon wasn't really a part of it. I would hang out with them occasionally but still stick to my own friend group. However, Carly and I started to get on each other's temper and joke around; it was really interesting because that's never happened to us before, but it could also be that we're hanging out with each other more.

"I'm taking a break just like you thank you very much." Carly squinted at me.

"Hey, I'm only taking a break because of everything Saylor and I have been through, our lives are crazy right now," I stated my case.

"Were, past tense. As far as I know, from what Saylor has said you're all healed. *Cough cough* not to mention her 18th birthday." Carly corrected.

"Are the other girls like this to you?" I asked turning to Devon, purposely ignoring the last sentence.

"No, but I'm mainly scared of them, but I must say, your girl scared me when we were freshmen. I can tell that she's changed a little bit." Devon answered.

"It's because she's been around Taylor and had to change her name. But I didn't think that a different name would change her at all. Maybe it was because of her parents but I don't know." Carly cut in.

"Could be more of her parents." I sighed, putting my head in my hands. Still wondering what is so important that my dad wanted to see me about. Was my Peppermint still in trouble? Was Scarlet someone I should never trust and she should just stay out of the way? What does he have to say about her? The thoughts that were always at the back of my mind.

"What? What's wrong?" Carly went into a protective mode.

"How much do you know about what we've gone through these last few months?" I wondered.

"Every little detail, every little detail that I wanted to fly myself here just to put Saylor in my arms and tell her everything will work out and she'll survive." Carly spat out, continuing. "I wanted to help her get out of bed so she wouldn't be staying in bed all the time."

"Why do you call each other twins again?" I questioned.

"We look the same, our birthdays are two months apart, and we kinda used to act the same. We were the troubled ones in the group." She replied with. "We were also really close, her leaving left me in tears for several days. I didn't want to get out of bed, I was lucky to have Rachel and Lola." Her eyes were starting to get watery.

"I'm sure that's part of the reason why you wanted to come here, you knew how it felt to want to stay in bed and cry." I frowned. "Gosh, if only I could've stayed in touch with you guys. Curse my dad for making everyone get new phones and new phone numbers."

"Mhm, and don't blame yourself Stark," she nodded, closing her eyes.

Devon and I both had the same idea, we got out of our seats and went up to give her a hug. Then I stopped so that Devon could comfort her. I left them and went out to the backyard. I listened to the birds chirping and the leaves rustling against the wind. Today was going to be the day where I tell my Peppermint how much she means to me.

"So, what did you want to tell me?" Saylor asked. We were on the hill on my tailgate of the truck; Saylor was sitting on the edge with her feet dangling off, while I was standing on the ground in front of her.

"Saylor, my Peppermint, my savior." I started. "You've changed me in ways that I never thought was possible. We've been up and down, telling me things that you probably never told anyone else."

"Mhm." She nodded.

"I love you so much! You have no idea how much you mean to me." I put my hands on her hips.

"I love you too." She smiled, putting her hands around my neck.

"I made a promise to you that I was never going to leave you, I made a promise to you and your brother that I was going to protect you." I took a deep breath in then out as I continued. "I will always keep those promises. So, as I stand here with the most beautiful view and the most extraordinary, magnificent, gorgeous girl."

"Stark, what are you doing?" She wondered as I moved my hands from her hips and went down on one knee in front of her.

"Will you, Saylor Alexis Martez-Larren, marry me?"

Bella/Saylor:

"Wh-what?" I gasped.

"Saylor, will you marry me?" He repeated.

"Yes." I nodded, biting my bottom lip as I felt tears of joy and overwhelming feelings roll down my cheeks.

"Yes?" Stark repeated.

"Yes!" I cried out, jumping off the tailgate and going to the ground with him, and giving him a hug.

"I knew I had the bestest girlfriend." He put his arms around me and squeezed me.

"Fiancée now." I leaned away, grabbed the box that the ring was in, and took the ring out placing it on my finger. It was a silver phoenix with an orange carnelian crystal in the middle. I held out my hand to see what it looked like on me.

"The color matches your eyes, the phoenix is the tattoo you have. What do you think? Does it fit? Do you like it?" The way he was looking at me was the same way he was looking at me after graduation when I was trying to figure out what his expression was.

"I love it! And yes it fits." I turned myself all the way around and gave him a kiss on his head, then cheek, then lips, lastly the neck.

"Good."

"So, what do we do now?" I asked. We were curled up in blankets on the tailgate. I was wearing Stark's shirt and my undies, while Stark had his pants on.

"Well, first we tell people, then we plan, and are we going to have a bachelor and bachelorette party?" Stark explained.

"Sure," I replied with.

"Alright, so we also plan for two parties too. Or we let our friends take over that."

"Let's have our friends take over that."

"Okay, so that would be it. Should we start planning now?"

"Nah, tomorrow. I'd rather spend the night here with you."

"Okay, fine by me."

CHAPTER

8

Stark:

"Are you ready to visit dad?" Mia wondered, I was the only one going to see him. My mom, Saylor, Mia, and I were all in the dining room eating breakfast, today was going to be the day I visited my dad.

"A little, I don't want to go, but I am. It bugs me that he wanted to tell me something important about Saylor," I explained.

"Mom, do you know what he has to say?" Mia looked over at our mom.

"I do not, the officer said that your father begged on his knees just to be able to call me," my mom shook her head.

"What is so important?" Saylor questioned, it seemed she didn't get it.

"We don't know but what if you're still in danger?" I looked over at her.

"I'm not in danger Stark," she rolled her eyes.

"What about Scarlet? Hm?" I was starting to get upset, but I wanted to try to keep my calm. I already saw my mom and sister get out of their seats and leave.

"Scarlet, really? That's what you came up with? I'm actually not surprised." I didn't like the tone she was using, it was like a sarcastic tone.

"Yes, I don't like her and I don't trust her near us, or our family." I pushed.

"You don't have to like her or trust her! I do! She helped me! Taylor feels safe with her!" She wasn't necessarily yelling at me, but she was starting to raise her voice.

"She helped you? If anything Taylor did! You could have had Taylor grab a security guard! All Scarlet did was ask if you were okay! The guard could have done that after taking care of the guys!" My voice was starting to raise.

"Well, I was scared! I was freaking out and I didn't know what to do! So I did the first thing I thought of and that was having Taylor go and grab somebody! You know how scared I was, you felt it!"

"You're right, I did. But it still doesn't change anything," I relaxed, a little.

"Why not?!"

"Because! I don't like her! I don't trust her! And I know that you accepted that, but she gives me an off feeling and I don't want you around her." I yelled, but then calmed my voice.

"I can tell, you want me all to yourself. Selfish." She calmed her voice too, but there was still that hint of fire.

"That is not true and you know it!" I barked, while she flinched.

"Maybe you are like your father." Her sentence sank as she said each word. The whole sentence felt like a slap in the face, my cheek red and burning afterwards.

"I love you, but I need some time to myself," I calmed myself all the way down. Realization finally caught up to her.

"Stark," she muttered. "I..."

"I know," I nodded as I walked to my room.

"Stark!" She yelled, her words from before still stinging.

"Peppermint, I love you. But it hurt." I whispered, knowing that she could hear me. I went into my room, closed my door, and then laid on my bed, my back towards the door.

I didn't want to be my dad, I wasn't. But yet, I always think about it. I get my anger and yelling from him. We argued and yelled everytime we were around each other; I'm so used to yelling when I am mad or upset. What if, whenever Saylor and I are arguing, I yell at her, and she flinches like she did? What if she is right, maybe I am like my dad. She doesn't deserve someone like that...

A knock at my door interrupted my thoughts, which was probably good. The knock was followed by her voice.

"Stark? I'm sorry," I heard the door open then close.

"It still stings babe."

"I'm sure. I'm really sorry."

I stayed silent.

She sighed, "I was upset, we both were. I shouldn't have said what I said. It was wrong, I know how you feel about him. I understand if you don't forgive me right away, but I'll be here for you, even when you ask me to leave. I love you Stark."

Her voice was soothing, calming, comforting, but there was also a bit of sadness. It was my turn to sigh as I rolled over to face her and sat up.

"I took care of the breakfast dishes," she gave a small smile, though it didn't match her eyes.

"In every relationship there will be disagreements, arguments, yelling, but hopefully at the end of the day you still love them. Peppermint, you were half right about one thing. I do want you all to myself, but I also love seeing you hanging out with your friends and family. I am not selfish, and you know that. I've told you that there are only three females that can take up my heart. My mom, my sister, and my Peppermint." I explained.

She stood there in the middle of my room, bottom lip trembling, trying to keep herself from crying, her eyes were closed.

"Babe, open your eyes, come here." I held out my arms as she opened her eyes and came over to me. I scooped her up, holding her tightly against me.

"I'm sorry," she mumbled.

"You're forgiven. Like you said, we were both mad and upset. I love you and that will never change," I told her, giving her a kiss on her forehead.

She looked up at me and we leaned into each other, a kiss, sweet and tender. I moved her so that she was laying on her back while I hovered over her.

"Ready?" She wondered. We were now in the car at the police station. Saylor was dropping me off and was going to be picking me up as well.

"Yea, I'm going to be in then out. I'll let you know when I'm done," I told her.

"Stark," she sighed.

"Yes?" I asked, I had a feeling what was coming to me.

"He's your dad. You may not like him but if he tries to have a conversation with you, then let him. But make sure you still get what you want out of visiting him though," she explained.

"Of course, I'm going to get the information! It has you in it, and it's important! What if you're in more danger?!" I exclaimed.

"Chill Stark. Just please let him talk to you, let him say whatever he wants to tell you," she was calm.

"Okay, I will," I agreed.

"Promise?"

"I thought you didn't like promises,"

"Stark, please," she begged.

"Okay, I promise," I said seriously.

"Thank you, I love you," she smiled.

"Love you too," I smiled back and gave her a kiss on the cheek.

"You should go," she advised.

"Alright," I gave her one more kiss, on the lips this time and got out of the car.

When I entered the building there were chairs, desks, and of course many officers.

"How can I help you?" The first lady at the desk asked.

"I'm here to see Mr. Hunt, my dad." I answered.

"First and last name please,"

"Stark Hunt."

"Right this way," I followed an officer that came over to us. We walked all the way down a hallway until we reached a door. The officer opened the door, nodded me in, and as I walked in, he informed, "We'll send your dad in. When you're done you can just leave."

"Sounds good, thank you." I thanked, sitting down in the chair. An officer and my dad soon came in, my dad in handcuffs.

Saylor being the only reason I'm here, I said, "I don't want to be here."

"Nice to see you too kid," he laughed leaning forward on the table.

All I did was squint my eyes at him.

"I'm glad you're here," he sighed.

"Why? It's not like you see me every day, why are you glad I'm here? I'm only here for one reason, and yet you haven't told me yet."

"Look, I was trying to keep my job and make sure that you, your mom, and your sister all had a home. Even if I wasn't in the picture, I still care about you all," he explained.

"Really? I find that hard to believe," I rolled my eyes.

"I messed up, I know. I heard about you and Saylor, congrats, you seem a lot happier with her," he sat up more and tried to have a conversation with me. I sighed and thought back to what Saylor told me.

"Yea, she's pretty cool," I nodded.

"Mhmm," he rolled his eyes like he didn't believe me.

"She is." I started to get upset, how was I supposed to stay calm? How does Saylor do it?

"I know, I know. Chill. But, she has to be more than 'pretty cool' if you were to risk your own life for her," my dad agreed.

"She is, she's the best," I mumbled, looking off to the side.

"And you care a bunch about her," my dad led on.

"Yes, of course. I'd get shot again if I had to save her again," I cleared my throat. Why was it that I was getting sad about this? The tears were coming, and I didn't cry often, unless it did come down to Saylor. The feeling from a few months ago came, I couldn't ignore it, I stood up.

"Stark! Where are you going?!" My dad started to shout.

"Saylor! She's in trouble again, isn't she? That's what you wanted to tell me. And great! Guess what! I'm going to save her! Where is she right now?!" I started to yell at my dad.

"She's with Scarlet, I wanted to make it up to you for being a horrible father. I'm sorry Stark," my dad sighed, leaning back in his chair.

"Where's Scarlet, do you know where?" I asked calmly.

"Call Andrew, tell him about the Phoenix organization. He'll know exactly where to go. But you have to hurry. I'm sorry Stark, I am. I was going to tell you sooner, I didn't realize she meant so much to you." He explained. I was starting to walk out of the room while he was apologizing, but turned half a step around when he said the last part.

"Dad, we're engaged. I told you I was going to marry her. Did you not think hard enough then? Or realize it sooner?" Tears were in my eyes, my stomach hurting more, more than when she was at the mall with my dad.

"Go save her. Put Scarlet in jail too."

Bella/Saylor:

When Stark left the car I decided to drive around. Find some place to relax and think. I soon found a place where nobody was around. A doc with the ocean, not a lot of boats. I parked my car and walked up to the doc, breathing in the fresh air.

Then I heard someone approaching, but I decided not to look back. When I did and noticed, it was Scarlet.

"Hey girl!" Scarlet smiled and nudged my shoulder.

"Hey, how's Taylor?" I asked.

"She's good, better than you," she shrugged.

"That's good, wait, what?" I didn't comprehend that last part and when I turned to face her, she took the apple she had, shoved it in my mouth, and plugged my nose.

"H-e-y! S-c-a-r-," I tried to muffle out.

"Shut it you!" She took hold of my arm and pulled me somewhere.

"Wake up!" Scarlet snapped.

"Whe-re am-m I?" I stuttered out while opening my eyes.

I looked around the room I was in. It looked like a basement with concrete floors and walls. There were a few lockers, benches, and a table. Scarlet wasn't alone, she also had three other people with her as well. When I tried to move I couldn't, my wrists were tied to the back of the chair.

"Sweetie, don't panic. You're safe with us, I promise," Scarlet smiled.

"I trusted you! My niece felt safe with you!" I yelled.

"Can you make her quit yelling?!" One of the people yelled, it was a male's voice.

"Saylor, pumpkin, it's ok. We just want to see your blood type, that's all we're gonna do." Scarlet came over to me and bent down in front of me.

I tried to concentrate on my powers, but it seemed so hard. I haven't practiced since Stark got put in the hospital. Even then I was weak for a few days.

"Honey, you can't use them. I put a little antidote so that you can't use them on us," Scarlet put her hand on my shoulder.

"On us?" I quoted.

"Yes sweetie," she nodded clueless.

So, I'm eligible to use them, just not on her or the other people? I concentrated again, trying to get myself free. If I couldn't, then she worded her sentence wrong and she took away my powers. But, I looked into her eyes, letting my anger try to burn my hands up so I could burn the ropes.

"What is she doing?!" The same voice from before asked

"I don't know, but we better get that blood, we need to get enough of it so she'll be weak," Scarlet moved away from me and to the table.

My hands were finally heating up where I could burn the ropes. When Scarlet came back to me with a needle I was free, when she held it up close to my skin I moved and smacked the needle out of her hands.

"What was that?!" Another man screamed. Terror washed through me. Stark, where are you?

"I don't know!" Scarlet ran for the needle as I burned the ropes around my ankles.

"I thought she couldn't use her powers! You said we were safe!" A woman yelled.

"That's because she said 'on us'. Which means, I could still get myself free." I stood up on the chair and crossed my arms.

"You rascal!" Scarlet looked up at me, needle in hand.

"Saylor! Are you in here?!" I heard Stark's voice from a long hallway.

"Yes! But Stark, be careful!" I warned getting off the chair.

"I think you forgot something honey," Scarlet came in front of me, putting her hand under my chin.

"Ahg!" Stark mounded. I looked around the room, nobody had moved, why was Stark in pain?

"Babe?! What's wrong? Are you okay?" I kept my eye in Scarlet's hand but also looked towards the hallway to see Stark kneeled down on one knee.

"Peppermint, how scared are you?" He muttered out.

"Scared? What does that have to do with anything?!" I questioned, panicking.

"Don't worry about it, I'll deal. I just want to keep you safe and protect you." It made me ache when he tried to stand back up, when he did get up, the pain on his face made my heart drop. Was I causing this?

"Get him, kick him in the gut. Make him bleed." Scarlet snapped at the others.

"No." I turned my attention back to Scarlet. Feeling my phoenix shine through, which I didn't know how it was possible.

"Excuse me?" Scarlet tilted my chin up.

"No." I repeated, this time I took my hand, grabbed her wrist, and twisted it, to the point where I make have broken it, or dislocated it.

"Hey!" Scarlet tried to twister her own hand back to normal, it was strange to see.

My own self surprised me, "you're lucky we want you alive."

I let go of her hand and acted fast, too fast for me. It was like I was the flash. I took her and put her in the chair I was in. I tied her wrists and ankles to the chair just the way I was tied. I took the needle and put it back on the table.

"Ugh!" I heard Stark groan in pain. I was too busy dealing with Scarlet; I didn't pay any attention to Stark. I looked over and noticed that Stark was pretty beatin', and badly.

"Hey!" I shouted over at them, "Would you like to end up like Scarlet? Or worse? Quit messing with my fiancé!"

They looked over at Scarlet, to me, then back to Stark.

"Finish them!" Scarlet told her group and they listened.

One continued to beat Stark while the other two came after me. I looked over at a pipe and wished that it could hit one of them, or both of them. To my surprise, the pipe started to lift in the air and then it hit both of the people, knocking them to the ground. They probably got a concussion, the pipe soon dropped and landed on her ankles.

"Ouch, that's gonna leave a mark," I cringed feeling back to my normal self.

"Ahg!" Stark coughed out.

"Leave. Him. Alone!" I ran towards the last person, jumped up, and tackled him. His head also hit the concrete, leaving another person in a concussion.

"Pepp-er…" Stark mumbled.

"Stark?" Worried, I looked over to where Stark was laying on the ground, his face all bloody.

"H-hey," he attempted to smile.

"Don't talk, let me help." I rushed over to him, trying to get him to sit up against the wall.

"Your… Brother… Should." He closed his eyes, the pain was too much for him.

"No, not again. Please don't leave me," I cried, biting my lower lip.

Then he started to laugh, a small chuckle.

"What? What could you possibly be laughing at?!" I yelled.

"We're a mess Peppermint," he opened his eyes, he still looked weak.

"You promised you weren't going to leave me," tears were running down my face.

"And I won't beautiful," he lifted his hand to my face and wiped my tears away.

"Saylor?! Are you down here? We have the cops." I heard Andrew's voice from the hallway.

"Yes! Come here!" I yelled. I looked back at Stark, his eyes were closed again, he was still breathing. "Stark, can you tell me something? Just, so I know you can hear me."

"I promised…" He gasped for breath. "That I would protect you. And I intend to keep that damn promise."

"Stark…" My lip was trembling as more tears went down my face.

"We're going to get married next month, have a small ceremony. We'll be safe then, your brother and the cops will find everyone who works with this organization, and then we'll be safe. You will be safe.

71

We can live a happily ever after. Of course, we'll need to find a house, which I'm sure our family would help with. I'll get a part-time or full-time job while you do online college. Everything will turn out fine." Stark opened his eyes again, a faint whisper as he explained.

"Mhm," I nodded, my lip still trembling, holding onto his wrist that was still on my face.

"I love you."

"I love you."

"Saylor! Stark! Are you guys okay?" Andrew ran over to us, cops and nurses with him.

"Stark isn't, he's beaten and bloody. I'm alright, crying, but that's all. There are three unconscious people, two men, one woman. Scarlet is tied up in a chair." I explained, looking up at Andrew.

"Get four paramedic beds." Andrew looked at the nurses who nodded and left. Then looked to the cops, "the girl you want is tied up in the chair." Then to me, "how tightly did you tie her up?"

"So that she wouldn't escape, if you want me to, I can burn the ropes." I answered, looking over at Scarlet.

"We'll see what we can do, and if we need you, we'll let you know." One of the officers told me before they both went over to untie Scarlet.

"Andrew, is Stark going to the hospital again?" I looked at my brother with a desperate look.

"Yes, but he should be out in a week," Andrew answered then went down on the floor with us.

"Hey Andrew," Stark tried giving a small smile.

"Hey Stark, good job once again. How are you doing?" Andrew gave a small smile back to him.

"I'm alright. They kicked my gut a few times, threw a couple punches. But your sister is pretty good at fighting," Stark explained.

"How's breathing? And yea, she's pretty good," Andrew wondered, then looked over at me.

"It's alright," Stark coughed out.

"Coming through!" One of the nurses yelled.

"I'm going to go see if the policemen need me and then I'm coming back over here. I'm going with you." I stood up and held onto Stark's hand.

"Okay, see you soon," Stark nodded.

I let go of his hand and walked over to them, "need any help?"

"We should be good," one of them said.

"Okay," I took a deep breath in then out and ran over to Stark who was on a paramedic bed with Andrew on one side of him. Once I got to them I looked over at Andrew and asked, "hey, while I was freeing myself from Scarlet, a whole different side of me came out. Could that have anything to do with my powers?"

"Well Saylor, yes, you probably have a few more powers as well. You'll keep getting more of them, there are only ten. You will keep getting them as you get older." Andrew answered.

"Huh, thanks for the information," I thanked.

"Yea, I should have told you sooner," Andrew nodded.

"Well, it's okay. What matters right now is Stark being okay," I looked down at Stark and gave a small smile.

CHAPTER

9

Stark:

"Hey babe," I put my arms around Saylor's waist, resting my chin on her shoulder, seeing what she was up to.

"Hi," she sighed, leaning back into me.

"Whatcha up to?" I asked, we were in her dining room with papers and a big binder all over the table.

"Making sure that everything is set for the wedding," she leaned forward, looking at one of the papers in her hand.

"The wedding is in three days, not including today," I told her, noticing how tired and stressed she looked. "You need to relax and take a break for once. You've been planning this a week after I got back from the hospital. When was the last time you took a break and pushed it to the side?"

"One, I've gotten help planning our wedding, so it's not just me. And two, everytime I go to bed I get a break from it."

"One, I know. Two, that doesn't count. You stay up until eleven, get ready for bed, and then go to bed. When you wake up, you get ready for the day and then get back to work on our wedding again."

"Fine, but don't you have a bachelor party to get ready for?" She gave in, but changed the subject.

However, I was in no mood for a subject change, "Saylor."

"What?!" She sighed, showing how high her annoyance was starting to get. Though with her sleep schedule, this wasn't new.

"Turn around, and face me," I lifted my chin off her shoulder.

"What?" She turned around to face me and crossed her arms.

"You need to take a break," I repeated in a different way.

"I will! At some point!" She cried out. I held her close to me, wrapping my arms all the way around her, holding her in place tightly.

"Go to bed at eight, I'll tell you about my bachelor party in the morning. After that, you're sticking with me until your bachelorette party. No wedding stuff." I explained, having my voice a little stern.

She looked at me like it was the best thing she's heard all day today. Her eyes looked like she was about to cry and she hadn't blinked for a bit. She nodded and blinked a few times as the tears went streaming down her face.

I sighed and pulled her into me. Holding her tightly as she rests her head on my chest. I put my chin on the top of her head as she wrapped her arms around me. I gave her a kiss on the top of her head, taking in the scent of her strawberry conditioner.

"I'm sorry for acting how I did," she apologized, leaving back and wiping her eyes.

"It's ok, I'm sure it's just wedding jitters," I smiled and gave her a kiss on her forehead.

"Are you nervous? Or anxious?" She wondered.

"Only a little," I shrugged.

"What?!" She gasped, making me laugh.

"I'm sure I'll be terrified on our wedding day. By the way… can I see a sneak peak of the dress?" I smiled, hoping to see it.

"No." She shook her head. "It's bad luck to see your fiancé in her wedding dress before she walks down the aisle."

"Bad luck?" I teased.

She squinted her eyes at me before saying, "In Grey's Anatomy Alex saw Jojo in her wedding dress before she walked down the aisle. Then they ended up in a mess and are no longer together. However, the actor who played Alex didn't like how they started doing the shows, so he quit."

"And this is a TV show?" I hinted.

"Yes, but that doesn't mean you're seeing my dress."

"A TV show?"

She squinted her eyes at me again, "don't you have a party to get ready for?"

"Not really. Devon and I are going over to Landon's house and chillin'," I answered.

"When are you leaving?"

"As soon as I get a kiss on those lips," I smiled

She smiled as she rolled her eyes and leaned in to give me a kiss, "happy?"

"I think I need one more," I started to kiss the side of her neck.

"You're gonna be late."

"The party only starts when the groom arrives. Plus, Landon said we could go over whenever," I told her, still kissing her neck.

"I need to make sure the wedding is all set," she said as I slid my hands under her shirt. It was amazing how well she was able to hold herself together.

"The wedding is just about ready, once Devon comes back from the beach I'll go. For now, you're mine and you need a break from all of this," I told her, sliding her shirt off.

"I thought Devon was still here?"

"I sent him off to see Carly before the party. I told him to come back in an hour or two." I explained lowering my kisses down to her chest then her stomach. I stopped when I got to her waistband, "May I?"

"If we can go upstairs to my room," she answered.

"Mhm," I nodded and picked her up by her legs first; making her hang upside down and legs in the air.

"Stark!" She scowled, "don't forget my shirt at least!"

"I got it," I grabbed her shirt then started walking up stairs to her room.

"Did you even say a specific time for Devon to come back at?" Saylor asked, we were tangled up in the blankets and sheets, our clothes on the floor.

"Not really, just an hour or two. Why?" I answered making shapes on her shoulder.

"Just curious, that's all," she shrugged.

"Okay,"

"Stark?"

"Yeah?"

"I'm going to be right back," she got out of bed, grabbed her bathrobe and left the room.

"Okay," I mumbled, putting myself on my back. It took her a few minutes before she came back and collected her clothes.

"I'm going to be in the shower. Everyone just showed up, you should get dressed and ready to go," she explained.

"Hey, you alright? You were gone for a bit." I wondered, she was starting to act hella strange.

She gave me a smile, one I've never seen before, "yea, I'm good."

"You sure? You're acting a little weird," I eyed her suspiciously as I was getting my own clothes on.

"Yes! I'm okay!" She laughed, giving me a kiss on the forehead. "Devon is waiting for you."

"Alright, don't forget to go to bed at eight. I love you, see you in the morning," I said, getting out of her room and walking to meet with Devon.

"Ready to go?" Devon asked, his car keys in hand.

"Yea," I nodded. We walked out of the house and to his car, we chatted for a little bit, but my mind couldn't stop thinking about Saylor and how she was acting before I left. My stomach didn't hurt, which was good, but I was still worried about her.

When we finally got to Landon's place Landon greeted us with a hug and got us all settled in. That was when the questions started coming up.

"Are you ready to get married?" Landon asked.

"Yeah, I think so." I nodded.

"Do you know if Saylor is?" Devon asked this time.

"Good question!" I smiled, a big fake one.

"Wait, what does that mean?" Landon's eyes went wide.

"Well, she's been worried about the wedding and making sure it's perfect. I was finally able to get her to take her mind off of it, but before I left she was acting hella weird and strange. It's making me start to worry about her. So, I have no idea how she's doing right now." I explained.

"Man, women, girls preferably, are so confusing. It's a good thing I'm not interested in girls," Landon sighed.

"Wait, you're gay?!" I exclaimed.

"Yea, I figured I'd tell you one way or another," he shrugged.

"Congrats man," I smiled, giving him a pat on the back.

"Thanks," he smiled.

"Congrats, that's huge," Devon also congratulated him, but soon went back to the topic, "girls aren't too confusing."

"I guess, my sister is every so often. But, hopefully I won't have to worry about my so when I get to that point. For right now though, I'm happy to be single," Landon smiled leaning back in his chair.

"Alright buddy, you'll feel that way at some point," I laughed.

Bella/Saylor:

"So, it's positive?" I asked, unsure of what would happen next.

Sabrina, Andrew and I were sitting on the bathroom floor; it had been a few hours since Stark left and everyone showed up. I waited until dinner was over to figure out if my gut feeling was right or not. We had Rachel, Lola, and Carly watch the younger girls and keep them company while I was doing this, though they didn't know why exactly.. I didn't want anybody knowing because one, I was unsure and two, I didn't know if I wanted to tell Stark first or not.

"Yep," Sabrina nodded, handing me the two tests I took. One of them having two red lines and the other straight out saying 'positive'.

"Did you know this was going to happen?" I asked Andrew, who was being very supportive through this whole process, including when I called him.

"The thing about being the oldest sibling in a Martez family, is that when you turn 13 and a half you get to see snippets of your younger siblings' lives when they're older. However, very rarely, the future could change." Andrew explained.

"So, yes?" I guessed.

"Yes, how are you doing? Are you okay?" He questioned.

"I'm trying to comprehend all of this. I'm worried about what everyone is going to say, let alone what Stark will say. I'm also kinda scared too," I answered.

"Everything will be ok, we'll be here every step of the way," Sabrina comforted.

"Thanks," I gave a small, weak smile.

"Of course, do you know if it's one of us or not?" Andrew nodded.

"It is, it's the only way I knew that I was... Um... That I was," it was difficult saying the word. Sabrina and Andrew were looking at me concerned. "The gut feeling was the only way I knew I was having a child."

"We'll be here every step, for now, Stark wanted you to go to bed at eight?" Andrew gave a reassuring smile.

"Yea, he did," I answered, getting to my feet.

"Alright, well, good night sis. I love you," Andrew gave me a hug and then a kiss on my forehead.

"Love you too, good night," I gave a small smile.

I woke up the next morning rushing to my bathroom to throw up. I left the bathroom door open so when I heard his voice I jumped a little.

"I'm fine," I told him, flushing the toilet and rinsing my mouth out.

"You sure? You're not sick or anything?" He questioned.

"I'm fine," I repeated, deciding to brush my teeth.

As I brushed my teeth he stood in the doorway of the bathroom, watching me with a worried 'I don't believe you' look. He stayed in the doorway after I brushed my teeth and hair. Until I left the bathroom to go back into my room he followed me and sat down on my bed as I rummaged through my closet.

"Our wedding is coming up quickly," he informed.

"Mhm," I nodded, hoping that the shirt I picked wouldn't show the small bump I was already gaining. I realized that a Martez pregnancy was shorter than a regular pregnancy. A normal one would be 9 months, give or take a few weeks. A Martez pregnancy was roughly 6 months exact, my baby would be born on November 2; give or take only days.

"What happened to my stressing Peppermint?" He asked, he still didn't believe my 'I'm fine' answer.

"She disappeared," I answered, putting my bra that was already uncomfortable on, and taking off the oversized t-shirt.

"No duh Saylor," he was starting to get upset. I already had my shirt on and was putting my hair in a ponytail. Afterwards, I closed my door and went over to face him.

"I'm going through something, it's not just about our wedding now. It's something else, it's more important than our wedding. But it's..." I took a deep breath in then out. He was just sitting there, looking all hot and cute. He was in his sweatpants, no shirt, no socks, and his hair a mess. I took another deep breath in, then out. I felt the water forming in my eyes.

"Saylor, what's going on?" He asked, worried but serious.

"There's a new member to our little family," it was the only way I could have said it.

"What?" He was confused, did he not understand?

"Stark, I'm pregnant," I finally said, smiling and feeling the tears in my eyes. His expression changed a lot. Surprised, worried, confused, and then back to worried.

"How are you feeling?" He wondered, reaching out.

"Scared, nervous, happy," I gave a small smile and walked over to him. He wrapped my arms around me and put me in his lap. "How are you?"

"I don't know," he shrugged. "Terrified, but happy for us."

"Stark, I can promise you that you're not going to be like your dad." I put my arms around his neck and looked at him, knowing he probably had that on his mind.

"Thanks for the reassurance Peppermint," he smiled and then gave me a kiss on the cheek, forehead, the tip of my nose, and then lastly my lips.

"You're welcome, now, I was told that you had me until my party?" I grinned.

"Yes, what do you want to do?" He asked.

"Get ready for the say and then watch movies," I answered.

"Ok, then let's get ready," he confirmed. We soon finished getting ready and decided to have breakfast, even though I regretted it 10 minutes later. Once I was finished cleaning myself up, again, we snuggled on the couch and watched movies from Netflix.

"Are you ready to get this party started?!?!" Carly squealed, putting her arm around my shoulders. "We have cider, candy, popcorn, junk food, and pizza!"

Sabrina, Carly, Lola, Rachel, the younger girls and I were all i t hotel room. I had debated whether to have put Carly in charge of my bachelorette party or not, but if I was including my sisters and niece, I figured there wouldn't be any harm.

I smiled and took in the room, it seemed nice and big. There was a small kitchen, two bathrooms with showers, 2 beds, a couch, and a small table with some chairs surrounding it.

"Hey girls," I glanced at them all. Carly was in the kitchen getting stuff out of the bags with Sabrina, Rachel was flopped on one of the beds, Lola was looking out the window, and the younger girls were already jumping on the bed.

"Yes?" Carly smiled over at me, all the others looked at me too.

"I just wanted to let you girls know that I'm pregnant!" I bit my tongue and gave a small smile.

"Oh my gosh!" Carly and Lola both squealed, running over to me.

"Wait, are we going to be aunties again?" Alexis and Ella came up to me, a sparkle in their eyes.

"You guys already are, but yes, you have another nephew or niece," I smiled.

"What about me?" Taylor came running over.

"You're going to be a cousin," I told her.

"Wow," Taylor looked astonished. She knew very little about a family tree, but I know she knows her family tree vocabulary.

I laughed and looked over at Carly, "yes Carly, I'm ready to get this party started!!"

"Good! Cause we have one more thing to celebrate!" Carly beamed.

"I'm going to be the first to say this, but congrats Chica," Rachel sat up and smiled.

"Yes! Congrats!" Lola grinned.

"When did you find out?" Carly wondered.

"Last night while you older girls were keeping the younger girls occupied," I answered adding, "I told Stark this morning."

"So, I'm going to guess that Andrew knows too?" Lola guessed.

"Yea, Sabrina and him were with me when I was finding out," I nodded over to Sabrina who was looking over at us with a smile.

"Well, even though it's nice to hear about the child, it's time to party!" Carly changed the subject.

I laughed and we soon started to party. All we were doing was enjoying ourselves, having fun; we went swimming, had a pillow fight, and watched movies.

CHAPTER

10

Stark:

"Hey Peppermint," I brushed away a piece of her hair off the cheek, "Mmm," she mumbled.

"Come on, wake up. We need to get going," I told her as she opened her eyes.

"What time is it?" She asked, sitting up and checking her surroundings.

"Noon, Sabrina took you inside early this morning and you didn't want to get up to your room; so you passed out here on the couch," I explained.

"Oh, oh yea," she nodded sleepily like everything came back to her.

"How was last night?" I wondered, getting up and sitting next to her.

"It was fun, I told the girls about the baby, they were quite happy about it," she answered, resting her head on my shoulder.

"Come on Peppermint, we need to get going. We have the rehearsal dinner tonight, and then the girls are gonna take you from me. You can sleep in the car if you want," I rubbed her back.

"Okay," she nodded, sitting up. "It was fun, but I don't know if I'm ever going to let that happen again."

"Oh yea?" I laughed giving her a kiss on the forehead.

"Yea, I'm so tired," she was a little bit more alert but still really tired.

"Alright tired girl, come on, let's get up," I sat up and pulled her arms.

"Proper hug," she sighed, wrapping her arms around me.

"Wow, this is very different than it has been for a while," I smiled.

"I'm tired," she sighed, leaning away more lively.

"Okay."

We finally arrived at the beach house where our wedding was being held, it took us roughly an hour to get in the car because of how tired Saylor was.

"Man! What took so long?" Rachel sighed.

"You tired my girl out," I responded with nudging Saylor.

"Huh?" She perked up, still being a little unresponsive.

"You have not partied in a long time Saylor," Carly took her from me.

"Nope, I've been Bella and studying hard, plus I've been having other things than parties to do," Saylor answered, looking over at me.

"Hey, don't look at me, she took you from me," I held up my hands in defense.

"I know," she nodded.

"I have never seen her like this, so out of anything," Andrew informed, coming over to us.

"I blame them," Saylor pointed to her group of friends.

"Hey! We were having fun though," Lola whined.

"We were, we were," Saylor nodded.

"In my defense, I've never seen her act like this ever," I looked amused.

"Alright!" The marriage officiant, Tara, came out and announced, then looked over at Saylor, who was leaning on Carly. "What happened to our bride?!"

"It's been a good minute since I partied, so I'm a little out of sorts," Saylor answered.

"Ok, well, you need some caffeine." Tara took Saylor from Carly and walked away, to inside the beach house.

"She can't have too much!" I yelled, running up to them, though I saw everyone give me a weird look. "What? She can't have caffeine, I did some research last night."

"What is this research on?" Tara wondered, looking over at me when I went to them.

"Saylor's pregnant," I told her.

"Oooo, congratulations you two," she smiled, congratulating us.

"Thank you," Saylor and I thanked in unison.

"Well, I should guess you haven't had caffeine today?" Tara guessed.

"No, I haven't," Saylor answered.

"Okay, good." Tara nodded, getting her inside.

"Okay, this is how it goes people! Listen!" Tara yelled at everyone. After a few hours of Saylor getting her energy back, we started working on the wedding and how it would be. I was alone at the altar but I was still able to hear everything that was going on; though all the girls except Saylor and Sabrina were being goof balls, and messing around. "Guys! Come on," Saylor sighed, it was clear she wanted to be done and over with.

"Okay, okay, Alexis and Ella have to stop being funny with their walk though," Rachel couldn't stop laughing.

"Sounds like fun," my mom approached me from the side.

"Yea, I guess. Though, I'm with Saylor on this. I'm ready to spend the rest of the night with her until she gets taken away from me," I looked over at my mom who was holding a camera. "Mom, are you taking pictures of all of this?"

"Of course! I have to capture the practice rounds," she responded with a smile.

"Have you been taking pictures of bloopers too then?" I wondered, watching as Carly and Devon came walking down the aisle.

"Yes, they're some pretty funny ones, not going to lie," she beamed, walking towards Carly and Devon and stopping to take photos.

I moved to the right hoping to see Saylor, she was talking to Andrew and Sabrina about something. After all, they were the ones walking her down; I know it's been a struggle for her when it came down to who was giving her away since her parents were not here. Though she mentioned that she wanted Andrew to walk her down before they even said anything.

"Hey man," Devon lightly punched my shoulder and got to the left side of me.

"If that causes you guys to start all over again, I might as well kill you," I told him.

"Damn, we haven't seen each other in a while and you're already threatening me," he laughed a little.

"Aye, I just want to spend time with Saylor until she goes to bed," I laughed as well.

"Well, here she comes," Landon winked as he walked up next to Devon.

"Here she comes," I mumbled looking down the aisle. Even if she wasn't wearing a wedding dress she was still wearing a dress that looked amazing on her. The top of her dress had no straps and flowed down to her knees. All red with orange fire symbols on the bottom, the back of her dress only had a strap on the top for support and wrapped around to connect the skirt part.

The aisle seemed so long, which made the wait even harder, I can't imagine how tomorrow will be. The anticipation will be the death of me, though when I took her from Andrew, holding her hand was like destiny. I brought her up to the arch, facing each other and side-eying Tara. Hoping we got it all perfect for her, that we could end up starting the dinner party.

"That was amazing!" Tara beamed excitedly.

"Yay!" We all cheered, even if we hadn't done the vows and everything else before that; I kissed Saylor softly, and rested my forehead on hers, while I took my hand and held it up to her cheek.

"You ready for this?" She asked.

"Of course baby," I smiled. "Are you?"

"I can't wait," she mumbled, giving me a kiss.

"Alright guys, you had your moment, time to get dinner going," Carly sighed, happily though.

"Alright," I sighed, not wanting to let her go. She laughed and hugged me, looking over at Carly and the others who moved in front of us.

"Are you guys taking pictures?" She laughed with a question.

"No..." Lola mumbled sarcastically.

"Sure," she rolled her eyes then looked up at me, "come on, let's go eat."

"Alright," I let her go and held her hand. We walked down the aisle and got inside the building to get dinner.

"Okay, okay people," Tara began after everyone had their food and were sitting. "We'll have the couple mingle around, then food will be served to us. After a while everyone will eat, we'll do toasts and then more mingling and then when the couple is ready, we'll have our first dance from Andrew and Saylor then Stark and his mom, then the newlyweds dance, and everyone else will join them. After that, mingling and wishing the couple off to their honeymoon."

"That sounds great, thank you Tara," Saylor thanked.

"Of course," she smiled. Then looked at everyone again, "now, eat your food, we'll do toasts from the guardians, maid of honor, and best man. After, we'll practice some dancing, do a little bit of partying, and then bed!"

"Sounds good," I nodded.

"Yes, but not too late because we all need sleep for the big day," Tara said while eyeing the three girls.

"Fine," Rachel rolled her eyes.

"Good, I'm glad that's clear." I mumbled to myself, though Saylor heard me and side eyed me.

"You better get to sleep too then," she squinted her eyes at me.

"I will," I laughed.

"Good."

Bella/Saylor:

"Hey, it's time to get ready," Carly whispered, trying to wake me up.

"What time is it?" I grumbled rolling over to face her.

"9:30 in the morning," she chirped.

"Why so early?" I questioned, sitting up.

"Because we only have three hours to get you ready before your wedding," she answered, sitting up as well.

"I vaguely remember us sharing a bed," I yawned looking over at her, to where she was under the covers.

"Duh, where else am I supposed to sleep when the love birds took a kings size bed to themselves and with my boyfriend with your soon-to-be husband," she shrugged.

"How did they take up a king size bed??"I questioned, shocked.

"They can't sleep cuddling, or it was too hot that they were both sprawled out taking up the whole bed."

"Damn," I muttered, fully awake now. "Well, I guess it's time to get everyone ready."

"Okay!" Carly beamed and jumped out of bed.

I laughed and reached for my phone, seeing notifications from Stark.

Stark: Good Morning Beautiful. I can't wait to see you later. I want you to know that no matter what happens in our life we'll be doing everything together. Our baby will have an amazing mother, and I can't wait to find out if they'll be like you at all. I love you so much.

"Come on!!" Carly grabbed my arm and pulled me halfway out of bed.

"Okay, okay," I laughed getting out of bed.

"I'm going to go get the others!" Carly announced as she walked to the entryway and opened the door.

"Okay, sounds good!" I hollered back.

Once she left I headed to the bathroom to at least go to the bathroom, brush my hair and teeth. As I was brushing my teeth there was a knock at the door, I went over and opened it seeing Sabrina, Taylor, and my sisters all right there.

"Ready to start getting ready??" Sabrina smiled big.

I nodded in response as I still had my tooth brush in my mouth, I opened the door all the way to let them in. When they came in, the girls started putting their dresses on and insisted that they didn't need any help.

"We're here~" Lola sang walking into the room.

"In the bathroom," I called out.

"Ooo~ you're looking pretty," Rachel smiled walking into the bathroom, Carly and Lola following. Sabrina was just finishing putting my hair in a braid crown.

"Thanks I guess," I laughed. "I have to give Sabrina all the credit though."

"Now for make-up?" Carly suggested.

"No, I don't want to wear make-up," I told them, admiring myself. Then I started to get insecure and whispered, "Though I wish I could wear eye contacts."

"Hm?" Sabrina perked up, hearing a small portion.

"Nothing," I laughed off.

"Alright," Sabrina eyed me like she didn't believe me, but also waved it off. "Girls, ready to get her dress on?"

"Yesss~" Lola nodded excitedly running over.

Once we were all ready there was a knock at the door, Sabrina opened it and Andrew came in looking nice in his slick black suit.

"Wow Saylor," he muttered out.

"Thanks," I smiled.

"Well, are you ready to get married?" He asked, still stunned.

I looked at myself in the mirror, admiring my own dress. Mostly white, with an orange calm silhouette around the dress. The back was very open and closed once it got down to my hip. My veil was made of white tulle and a flowery orange crown held it together, the same orange that matched with the silhouettes.

"Saylor?" Carly wondered, which brought my attention back.

"Yea, I think I am," I nodded with a smile. I could almost feel the water coming from my eyes.

"Girls, after you. We'll follow," Andrew held the door open for everyone to follow. The ceremony was being held outside on the first floor. Our rooms were right by the area, there was no requirement to use an elevator or the stairs. All we had to do was walk down the hallway and turn to the left and there were the doors that led us to the canopy.

Andrew took my arm as we walked down the hallway. Nice and slow, and counting our steps so we weren't too close to my maid of honor, Carly.

"I can't believe it," I whispered to my brother.

"You're telling me sis," he smiled, nudging me.

"Were you nervous when you and Sabrina got married?" I asked.

"Oh, hell ya. I couldn't stop thinking about what her family would say with us getting married right after high school. Sabrina's friends thought I knocked her up." He explained.

"I know, I heard them talking about it," I sighed, recalling when my brother got married, her friends ended up pissing me off to the point where I had to leave early.

It wasn't until Sabrina noticed how tense Andrew was that she realized that they thought she was knocked up. Their wedding ended up being cut short because the more they talked about it and faked being happy for her, the more pissed Andrew got. Just like me, his hands also started to burn up as well.

"Saylor, we're next," Andrew snapped me back into reality.

"Right, we're next," I sighed, wanting to cry, wanting to be done and over with, wanting to run. I couldn't stand the slow pace we were walking, I just wanted to be next to Stark already, and kiss him, hug him, feel him, feel his touch.

"Breath silly," Andrew gave a small laugh as we started walking down the aisle.

"I know," I breathed out, not realizing I was holding my breath.

"Here's a bit of advice, keep your focus on Stark, and keep breathing. He's just as anxious as you are," Andrew advised, which he normally had good advice. I tried my best to breathe and keep an eye on him, I was smiling the whole way down, feeling the tears in my eyes come back.

"Hey baby," I heard him mutter. "You look beautiful."

I just smiled and kept myself breathing, Andrew kept talking me through a few things, telling me I was doing a good job.

"Stark, here is my sister. You better take good care of her," Andrew then handed me off. It felt like forever getting across the aisle just to be handed off to Stark.

"Of course," Stark nodded and took my arm.

"Hey," I smiled, soon getting to my position on where I had to be.

"Hey," he smiled back, then looked up at Tara who was about to start.

"Ladies and gentleman, family and friends. We are gathered here today to celebrate the beginning of two people finding their journey to each other. After this day, they will begin to find their way through life together, and as one. If anyone has any objects, speak now, or forever hold your peace." Tara announced, we waited silently for a short minute. It was all quiet which I believed was a good thing. Tara soon began looking from me to Stark, "Saylor and Stark have written their own vows that they would like to share with each other."

"I'll start," Stark nodded, getting out his piece of paper. "I didn't *fall* in love with you. I walked into love with you, with my eyes wide open, choosing to take every step along the way." He began, "I do believe in fate and destiny, but I also believe we are fated to do the things that we'd choose anyway." He paused and looked at me, tossing his paper to the ground, he looked at me, dead in the eye and finished, "and I'd choose you; in a hundred lifetimes, in a hundred worlds, in any version of reality, I'd find you and I'd choose you." His vow was done, and I was nearly about to cry.

"Oh god," I laughed a little. Then I got out my piece of paper, "Love isn't always perfect. It isn't a fairytale or a storybook." I began, wiping my tears. "And it doesn't always come easy. Love is overcoming obstacles, facing challenges, fighting to be together, holding on, and never letting go." I paused, looking up at him. "It is a short word, easy to spell, difficult to define, and impossible to live without." I started to cry, but continued, "love is work, but most of all, love is realizing that every hour, every minute, and every second was worth it because we did it together."

"Ah yes, the sweet emotional tears that come to every wedding," Tara smiled, looking from me to Stark, and then the audience, back to our ring bearer, Devon, "may we please get the rings?"

"Of course," he nodded and walked over in front of us. I took Stark's ring while he took my two, my wedding ring and then a promise ring.

"Thank you," Tara thanked while Devon walked back to his 'post'. "Saylor Martez-Larren, do you take Stark Hunt to be your faithful husband?"

"I do," I nodded, tears coming back to my eyes.

"Stark Hunt, do you take Saylor Martez-Larren to be your faithful wife?"

"I do," he smiled, squeezing my hands.

"Please place your rings on your left hand, on your ring finger," Tara instructed. Once we were finished, we looked up at Tara for the next step. "I hereby announce; husband and wife, Stark Hunt-Martez and Saylor Hunt-Martez! You may kiss!"

Stark let go of my hands and put them on my waist, pulling me close until our lips met. At first it was light and soft until I put my hands behind his neck and pulled him closer to me, deepening the kiss; making it hard and rough; still a very passionate kiss. It wasn't until we pulled away that I realized everyone was cheering, Andrew loud and clear. I couldn't help but laugh as I looked out into the crowd.

"Well, ready?" Stark asked, when I turned back to him.

"Yes!" I smiled.

"Let's go," he took my hand and we both walked down the aisle, everyone continuing to cheer.

"So, where are we going?" I wondered, as Stark started the car. The ceremony and after party was finally over, and I couldn't wait to rest. Though, I wanted our honeymoon to be a surprise, but now that we were hitting the road I wanted to know.

"I thought you wanted it to be a surprise?" He teased me.

"It has been, but now you have to tell me," I explained.

"I have to tell you?" He questioned.

"Yes." I nodded.

"Alright Peppermint," he smiled. "We're going to a private island."

"How did you afford that?!?" I gasped.

"My grandfather, and my own father," he answered.

"That was sweet of them," I smiled.

"Yea, it helps that my grandfather knows a guy."

"Yea, it does help. When was the last time you talked to your dad?"

"A few weeks ago, he's trying to make it better and change, but I'm still upset with him."

"Well, you're definitely going to be upset with him, but your life will be easier if you forgive him, you don't have to forget what happened, but forgive him so you can move on in life." I explained.

"Alright, when did you become so wise?" He glanced over at me.

"I don't know, I think I'm starting the mom brain," I shrugged.

"Cute, how's the little one doing anyway?"

"They seem pretty good," I smiled, rubbing my tummy.

"Can I ask if they're special or not?"

"I wouldn't call it special, but yea, they are," I sighed.

"Sorry," he frowned.

"It's okay," I comforted.

"If you say so," he gave a small smile.

"Yes," I beamed.

CHAPTER

11

Stark:

16 years later….

"Alright, what should we get for momma?" I asked my three children when we walked into the store, cart in hand.

"Flowers?" Our 15 year old, Alex suggested.

"Didn't we do flowers last year?" Bailey, the 13 year old, rolled her hazel nut eyes that she shared with me and her younger brother Charlie.

"So? We can always give your mom flowers, even if it's not a holiday." I smiled, looking over at Bailey.

"If you say so," she shrugged.

"Daddy knows so!" Charlie, who was seven, cheered.

I laughed and wondered," Should we get her anything else?"

"Candy!" Charlie looked at me wide-eyed excitedly.

"Yea, we can get her some sour patch kids, and the carmel geradelis," Alex agreed.

"Can we get mom some fluffy socks? Or a cute outfit?" Bailey asked.

"Sounds good buddy," I looked over at Alex and then to Bailey, "sure, we can get her a cute outfit."

"Yay!" Bailey beamed, a smile she shared with her mom.

"Ok, so, flowers, candy, and a clothing article?" Alex reviewed.

"That's what it sounds like," I nodded.

"Alright," Alex smiled. "I think mom's gonna like it."

"Of course she will! It came from us!" Bailey exclaimed.

"You're too cocky," Alex rolled his blue eyes. He didn't like feeling unique from others so he was able to convince Saylor and I to let him get blue eye contacts for him. Though it also led him to having to wear glasses as well.

"At least I have a normal appearance and I don't have to hide anything or be insecure about anything," Bailey shot back.

"Hey!" I gave Bailey a warning look. "And for the record, you do have to hide something."

"Sorry Alex," she mumbled, then looked at me. "Why can't I dress like mom dressed like when she was my age?"

"Because, grandma and grandpa had different views on what your mother wore compared to what I think is appropriate. You don't need to be showing off your tattoo. Even if you guys are no longer in trouble." I explained, a conversation that's been repeated many times.

"Ladies would go after that tattoo of yours though, same with the guys with mine…" Bailey remarked, then came a mutter at the end that I couldn't hear.

"Oh shush," Alex rolled his eyes at her, his good hearing definitely comes in handy especially when she mumbles and it could potentially get her into trouble.

"Heyyy! My man!" I heard a voice from behind me before I could've asked what she was saying. I looked back to see that it was Landon, a voice I've recognized for so long.

"Yo! What's up?" I smiled, pulling him into a 'man hug'. Then glanced at Alex and Bailey, who both knew this wasn't the end yet, "we'll talk about this later."

"Just getting more diapers for little Rosie, she's having a little blow out this week," he sighed looking over at his 5 month old daughter that he adopted not too long ago. "Everything good with you guys?"

"Aww, poor girl," I frowned, moving our cart out of the aisle. I then looked back to the kids, "everything is swell, just a little Martez thing."

"Ah, gotcha," he nodded.

"What are you guys doing for mother's day?" Alex asked quickly, wanting to move on from his powerful ears.

"Rosie and I will be going over to my mother's, we'll be meeting my sister there and having a little celebration," Landon smiled. "Thanks for asking buddy, what do you guys have planned?"

"All the aunties, except Taylor, are coming over. Plus Cody and Dove, Aunt Carly's kids. We'll be having a little barbeque," Alex answered. Then he took a minute to think about something and glanced over at me, "which, dad, do we have everything we need?"

"All we need to get is your mother's gift, Devon is taking care of everything. Plus Aunt Rachel and Aunt Lola are bringing side dishes." I told him.

"Ok, cool." He nodded, making a mental note in his head.

"Alright, well, have fun shopping, I got to get this little one going, and get something for my own mother before my sister kills me," Landon laughed.

"Bye man, nice seeing you," I waved as he started going off into the baby section.

"Daddy, can we get stuff for mommy now, I'm hungry?" Charlie whined.

"Yes, buddy, we can get mommy's stuff now. Maybe we'll stop somewhere to get food on our way home," I nodded.

"Yay!" All three of them cheered, as we continued walking.

Bella/Saylor:

"Baby, time to wake up," Stark whispered in my ear, rubbing my shoulder.

"Hmmm," I grumbled. "Do I have to? It's mother's day, why can't I stay in bed?"

"I'm sorry Peppermint, I'd let you, but it's already eleven in the morning and I've been distracting the kids all day. Plus, we have a party to get ready for, and there's breakfast on the table. I've already got the kids diving in on eating, and then gave Alex strict tasks for all of them to do some cleaning and set up." He explained, giving me a kiss on the shoulder that I had poking out from under the blankets.

"We have children?" I teased with a smile, rolling on my back.

"Yes, we have children," he laughed hovering over me.

"If only you liked morning breath," I frowned.

"For fifteen years on this day, I always have at least a kiss for morning breath," he smiled, leaning in.

"Oh shit, our oldest is fifteen?" I gasped, though I knew Alex was fifteen, though he didn't like what my side of the family carried, he was always my right hand man.

"My lord lady, are you already starting to lose your memory?" He joked, his lips inches from mine. Even after being married for 16 years, there was still the sexual tension, and heat that always lingered.

"Well, with three rambunctious children, it's not hard to happen," eventually I had to breathe, but I didn't want the gulp that I had to actually come. He laughed once more as he kissed me like no other. Sweet, gentle, and soft; everything that came with our relationship.

"Time to get up now Saylor," he pulled away and got off the bed.

"Come back?" I wondered, knowing I wasn't going to get anywhere.

"I'll see you down stairs," he smiled, coming to the other side of the bed, giving my forehead a kiss, and leaving the room.

"I love you," I whispered, also knowing that he wouldn't hear me.

I was prompted to get out of bed, but as I stared at myself in the mirror of the bathroom, I had a strange feeling. I always called this place my home, since the day I set foot after my parents died. Stark and I ended up getting the home I spent my important days in. Andrew and Sabrina gave us the house after Taylor decided to go out of state for college and they didn't need a big house any more. Especially since our apartment was getting too small for us, Landon reluctantly took the house with the fact that he was getting into the adoption process, where he finally found his baby girl a few years later. Stark and I did minor changes to the house, more so expanding the kitchen so it could fit everyone, we loved it when the kids helped out with dinner. By 13 Alex knew how to make Chinese food, and a 5 star course meal, we joked around that he would end up becoming a chef at his own restaurant one day, and he definitely took it to heart. He's been taking culinary classes and is now taking them at college level online.

"You're mean mom," I heard Alex whisper a few times, but didn't realize he wanted something out of it.

"I'm sorry kiddo, I do love you. And what did I tell you about tuning your ears out?" I apologized but soon turned back to my usually parenting style of being the mom but also the 'best friend'.

"You and Uncle Andrew need to teach me more, it's a lot of energy and practice,"

"Previously, you have to also find time to practice as well. You can't always count on us,"

"Alright," he sighed.

"Alright, now, help out your father, I'll be down soon." I smiled, though I knew he couldn't tell, but I knew he would by the sound of my voice.

By the time I made it down stairs to the kitchen the house looked spotless, toys were picked up and in their baskets we had out for them, the carpet was vacuumed, the countertops were spotless.

"It looks amazing guys!" I praised them, finding them all in the dining room. Bailey and Charlie were both coloring while Stark and Alex were playing Sudoku.

"Thanks mom," my older two thanked me, looking up at me.

"Thank you mommy, Daisy even got a bath!" Charlie beamed up at me, his face covered in chocolate milk.

"Stark, why haven't you noticed Charlie's face?" I asked, then said, "Charlie, go wash your face up before family gets here."

"Okay mom!" He chirped, jumping out of his seat and running to the bathroom.

"Sorry Peppermint, I forgot about it, he was persistent that Daisy got a bath that I completely forgot about it," Stark explained. Daisy was our German shepherd, she is about a year old now.

"It's ok," I smiled. I went over to Bailey and gave her a hug around the head.

"Mom! You can't look!" She then put the front half of her body on the table covering the drawing she was working on.

"Okay, okay, I'm sorry baby. I didn't mean to, I just wanted a hug." I frowned, apologizing.

She turned to look at me and smiled, "you could've just said something."

"Oh really," I laughed as we went in for a hug.

"Happy Mother's Day momma, I love you." She mumbled, hugging me tightly.

"Thank you sweetie, I love you too," I gave her a squeeze and made my way to Alex. "You don't have anything I'm not supposed to see right?"

"Nope, Uncle Devon and Cody are bringing it," Alex answered, giving me a hug. "Happy Mother's Day mom."

"Oh really?" I laughed, giving him a kiss on the top of his head. "Thank you kiddo."

"My turn, my turn," Charlie came running into the dining room, his chocolate face all cleaned up.

"Okay, okay," I laughed, picking him up and spinning him. "Man, you're getting heavy little man."

He laughed and gave me a hug, "Happy Mother's Day momma."

"Thank you," I nuzzled into him, his baby smell almost fading.

LITTLE BONUS....

Carly and Devon got married soon after Saylor and Stark. They had two kids, Cody whose 13 and Dove whose only 2. They have a cat named Kit, she is 11 months old and a Siamese mixed with gray tabby.

Rachel and Lola got married after some time of being open to the world. They decided traveling was the "greater good in life" and helping families all around the world. They have no kids or pets, but they think about getting a dog once they've settled down.

Landon is a happy, single dad who has joined the adoption center and adopted a beautiful African American baby girl, Rosie. Although he is living in an apartment now, he hopes to have a bigger house so he can foster kids who can't live a life at home.

Taylor has graduated from law and is now working her first case as her client is trying to sue their parents from abusing their power on their great uncle who was placed in their home after he had a stroke and had half his body paralyzed. Taylor has yet to meet the dating world, but when she does, she hopes to meet someone who could protect her Martez secret. The only animal she has is a gerbil, who is named Lesha.

Andrew and Sabrina have also took some time to travel but settled in near their daughter as Andrew tries not to hover over her. To prevent the hovering, Sabrina and Taylor both got him an eight week old cocker spaniel to take over his time, who was named Bella. Sabrina takes upon being a tour guide and learning new hobbies such as crocheting, bird watching, and helping people around her community.

Mia, Stark's younger sister, works as a judge with families in domestic violence. She has a boyfriend who is caring and just as sweet as she is. Stark has grown to like him, and realizes that he's good for her. She has one dog, a German shepherd named Connie and one cat who she rescued, a calico named Lucky. Connie is 2 years old, a female while Lucky is a month old, a male.

The big family, Saylor and Stark Hunt-Martez. They have three beautiful children; Alex whose 15, a full Martez, Bailey whose 13, half a Martez, and Charlie, 7 and is not a Martez. The only pet they have is Daisy, their German shepherd who is now a year old. Stark became a chief detective who spends most of his time looking for people who follow under the lines as an abuser, molester, or child kidnapping; though Saylor worries about him, she knows that they'll be just fine, and if anything does go wrong, they'll go through it together, and she knows just how strong Stark is. As for Saylor, she works at an emergency vet taking care of all the animals who stay overnight. The days both Stark and Saylor have agreed to take off include Friday nights and the weekends to spend time with the children. Other than that, Stark works during the day while Saylor works the night shift. Alex is determined to become his own version of Gordan Ramsey after a joke his family made, he is soon to turn it into a reality once he gets his first job as a front line chef at a diner. Bailey wishes she could be like her brother and have a plan with what she wants to pursue, but with reassurance from her parents and brother, she is ok with not having a plan momentarily. As for Charlie, he is just a kid, and clueless about life other than making sure Daisy gets cleaned every week, or every day if his parents let him.

www.ingramcontent.com/pod-product-compliance
Lightning Source LLC
Chambersburg PA
CBHW051852170626
46807CB00003B/1439